rule *of* night

rule *of* night

TREVOR HOYLE

POMONA

A POMONA BOOK P-002

Mad in England!

Published by Pomona 2003

1 3 5 7 9 8 6 4 2

First published by Futura 1975
Copyright © Trevor Hoyle 1975, 2003
Afterword Copyright © Trevor Hoyle 2003

Pomona Books
P.O. Box 50, Hebden Bridge, West Yorkshire HX7 8WA, England, UK
www.pomonasounds.co.uk

Distributed in the UK by Turnaround Publisher Services Ltd,
Unit 3, Olympia Trading Estate, Coburg Road, London N22 6TZ

A CIP catalogue record for this book
is available from the British Library

ISBN 1-904590-01-2

Set in 10 on 13.5pt Granjon
Typeset by Christian Brett

Printed and bound by Biddles, Guildford.

CONTENTS

For Dorothy, Dawn and Darryl — about time too. (1975)

ESTATE

FIRST THING YOU SEE WHEN YOU ENTER THE DARK mottled-green stairwell of Irvine Block on the Ashfield Valley Estate, Rochdale:

IF YOU GET
CAUGHT IN HERE
GOD HELP YOU
LOUSY SCUM

The walkways of damp grey concrete strike out in all directions, converging in boring perspective to a meeting-point in the misty distance. Puddles are scattered every few yards like pools of cold black ink. The concrete steps rising upwards from the stairwell are vicious: sharp serrated edges that need but a moment's unwariness —a slip or stumble—to bring a cracked shinbone or a split knee. On the bottom step—like the remnants of an alien creature— three smashed eggs, their yolks smeared and their shells trampled to fragments.

As winter approaches the Estate becomes a draughty hell, a place where gusting winds blow grit in your eyes. On turning a corner you find yourself literally stopped in your tracks by a solid wall of air. At nights the kids play on the open landings, a rail between them and the drop, or gather in screaming, chattering groups like excited starlings, chasing each other in endless circles past the anodised lift-doors and round the concrete pillars and past the lift-doors. There are Indians and Pakistanis and some West Indians in the flats, but mostly the tenants are Lancashire working people from the mills and factories. Once inside, behind their own front doors, they stay put; social intercourse here is virtually non-existent.

The builders of the Estate, Messrs Crudens Ltd of Midlothian, worked to a specification drawn up jointly by themselves and the Office of the Borough Architect and Planning Officer: 'lightweight internal partitions and boarded floors'—from whose walls Asiatic ladies with green faces now stare inscrutably down, and where facsimile Toledo swords, encrusted with bits of coloured glass, dangle on featherweight chains. But the original sin was committed in Sweden (the home of all that's best in modern design), for it was there that somebody had a brainwave and invented the Skarne industrialised building system using 'pre-cast concrete floor, roof and wall panels with dry linings to external walls'. Skarne: the name fits the system like a glove; spare, ascetic, emotionless, hinting at Nordic frugality. The beauty of the system is that it efficiently and hygienically disposes of the maximum number of human beings (in this case three thousand, five hundred and thirty-two) in the smallest space at the most economical cost with the minimum of fuss and bother. And not least—having once developed and perfected the system—it requires no further mental effort or imagination; neither does it necessitate the exercise of aesthetic sensibility, social concern, or moral responsibility. In short, it is painless.

. . .

Rochdale officially became a municipal corporation in 1856 when it was granted the Royal Charter of Incorporation. It was only thirty-three years before this, in 1823, that the Lord of the Manor, Lord Byron, had sold the manor (which had been in the possession of the Byron family for nearly three centuries) for the sum of £350. As John Roby records in his book *Traditions of Lancashire* published in 1831:

In the 39th of Eliz., Sir John Biron held the manor of Rochdale, subsequently held by the Ramsays; but in the 13th of Charles 1 it was reconveyed. The Byron family is more ancient than the Conquest. Gospatrick held lands of Ernais de Buron in the county of York, as appears by Domesday Book. Sir Nicholas Byron distinguished himself in the civil wars of Charles 1; and in consequence of his zeal in the royal cause, the manor of Rochdale was sequestered. After the Restoration it reverted to the Byrons. Sir John, during these troubles, was made a peer, by the title of Baron Byron of Rochdale.

Like most other East Lancashire towns Rochdale in those days, and for a century to come, depended on the cotton-spinning industry. The area was ideal for cotton because the dampness of the climate allowed the fibres to be stretched and twisted without breaking. And the people thereabouts maintained a tradition of dour and unremitting toil that was exactly what the mills needed.

The town gradually built itself up along the banks of the Roch, the river dividing the centre of the town neatly in two, spanned by several bridges. On a hill stood the Parish Church, the focal point of the landscape; at the other extreme was Packer Street, described in 1866 as 'a foul and noisome slum'. By the turn of the century the Council had decided to do something about the river, which was polluted by effluents from the mills, and in 1903 work began to cover it over. The project took twenty years or more and wasn't completed until 1926, giving Rochdale the distinction of having the widest bridge in the world: 1,460 feet.

The town's other major claim to fame was as the birthplace of the Pioneers' co-operative movement, started in 1844, a method of trading which established the basic principles of profit-sharing by customers and which became the model for co-operative societies throughout the world.

Most people, however, don't remember Rochdale either for its 1,460-foot wide bridge or as the place where the Pioneers was founded, but as the home of Grace Stansfield, a mill girl who became world-famous as the singer and film star Gracie Fields, born in a terraced house (now demolished), number nine Molesworth Street, on 9 January 1898.

If you should care to look at a map of the North of England you will see that Rochdale is one of a chain of industrial towns: Ashton-under-Lyne and Oldham to the south; Bury, Bolton, Wigan, St Helens to the west; and further north, Accrington, Blackburn, Burnley, Nelson and Colne. Rochdalians will tell you, understandably, that their town is different from any of the others, and for once their native pride is justified. Rochdale is different because it *looks* different: the geographical quirk of having a river running slap-bang through the centre of the town means that the Town Hall (an imposing mock-Gothic structure built in 1871), the banks, the building societies, the cinemas, the public houses—even the Empire Bingo Hall—must face each other at a respectable distance across a wide thoroughfare; there is space and light and openness, and some air to breathe, even if it is bad for the lungs. The planners and developers are powerless to build on the central reservation for fear of disappearing through a thin crust of tarmac and into the dark and gangrenous waters of the River Roch. And for this same reason the main thoroughfare of the town is not called High Street but The Esplanade. We should be grateful for such small mercies, especially when it is difficult to show any gratitude at all for the Ashfield Valley Estate, which cost £3,104,500, for which sum the Corporation received:

30 four-bedroom 6-person flats

234 three-bedroom 5-person flats
372 two-bedroom 4-person flats
316 one-bedroom 2-person flats
62 bedsitter flats.

The least that can be said is that it makes a change from Cayley Street with its two-up two-down, flagged back yard, outside lavatory, the square pot sink on iron legs in the kitchen, and in the mildewed front parlour the leaded windows looking out on to the street paved with irregular millstone setts — which is where the Seddons used to live. The house was in a long row with blue slate roofs close by the Rochdale-Manchester railway line and not far from the canal. At that time there were several mills nearby, which have since closed down or gone over from cotton to other industries such as light engineering, plastics or the manufacture of polyester foam. Most of the people in the district, then, as now, were manual workers, heavy drinkers, and tended to be short and stocky. They washed in the big white sink and occasionally had a bath in front of the fire. They ate (and still do) heavy lumpish food: potatoes, white bread, baked beans, suet puddings, fish fingers, shepherd's pie, and of course fish, chips and mushy peas.

The Seddons moved into the flats on the 18th February 1968, as soon as Irvine Block was completed (the Estate itself wasn't finished until February 1972). Now they inhabit cell number 472. Behind the flimsy door with its vertical strip of frosted glass you find yourself on a tiny landing from which a staircase on the left leads down to a passage that turns several right-angles, giving off to three bedrooms, kitchen, toilet, bathroom, and finally the living-room. It is like stepping underground, into a secret subterranean bunker, so the shock is that much increased when you look out of the window and find yourself thirty feet above ground — below you the concrete walkways and dilapidated flowerbeds and the flat roofs of garages neatly and symmetrically arranged. On one side, it is true, you have the undulating greenery of landscaped turf sloping down towards the Union Ring Mill, a sooty redbrick structure surrounded on three sides by the Estate; you might suppose that the planners forgot to remove it, or perhaps it was left there deliberately, in full view, as a reminder of the bad old days and the conditions folk had to endure before the arrival of post-war prosperity.

The visitor's first impression of the Seddon's flat is one of impermanence: the fabric of the place, no matter how well-appointed and decorated, reminds you of a motel room that appears to have been erected like a house of cards the moment you signed the register. The rooms are low, compact, utility boxes; the windows are small and regulation-height from the floor; the fittings, as you would expect, are mass-produced injection-moulded items that give the impression of having been designed for the benefit of the machines that made them instead of the people who are to use them: in the lavatory the warped plastic seat is split down the middle so that if you make a sudden careless move you find, if you're of that sex, your balls ripped off. The toilet cistern is also an Armitage product, and that too has a crack in the plastic casing from which the water continually seeps. Brian Seddon tried to mend it once with black insulating tape but the water still dripped and eventually the tape fell into the bowl and got flushed away. Another example: the doors in the flat and their frames seem to have been made by two joiners who bore each other a grudge. Some of the doors stick and during the damp winter months require a certain degree of force to open them, while others in the flat have gaps all round and open automatically with the pressure-wave of your approach. There are 1014 dwellings on the Ashfield Valley Estate and it would be an interesting, if futile, statistical exercise to discover how many of their doors fulfil the purpose for which they were intended.

The Seddons are a family of four: Brian, Margaret, Kenneth and Katrina. Brian and Margaret were married at eighteen (there's a four-month difference in their ages) and are now thirty-seven, which if you bother to work it out means they've been married nineteen years. Brian works at Turner Brothers Asbestos—or Turner & Newall as it now prefers to be called—the largest asbestos factory in the world and the biggest employer of labour in Rochdale. He's a service engineer in the maintenance section, a job he's had for almost seven years. Before this he flitted about, never staying more than a year or eighteen months with any one firm, finding it hard to settle down to a routine job; in his younger days he had been what they describe locally as 'a bit of a tearaway', and had dabbled amateurishly on the fringes of petty crime.

Margaret—except for the times when she was child-bearing—has worked all her married life, as waitress, chambermaid, barmaid and pub cleaner. Now she serves tea, coffee, meat pies and sausage rolls six days a week from ten till three in a snack bar on Oldham Road. They would be able to manage without her wage, but only just. With it they can afford to rent a colour television set and take holidays abroad: they've been abroad twice, in fact, on package holidays to Majorca and Benidorm. Brian would like a car and every Saturday looks at the classified columns in the *Rochdale Observer*, knowing full well that if he bought one the cost of running and maintaining it would curtail his drinking throughout the week and his and Margaret's nights out at the Kirkholt Social Club on Saturdays and Sundays. Brian does the pools each week with a syndicate of workmates, occasionally has a bet on the horses, and follows Rochdale Hornets rugby team.

So much for the background.

KENNY

KENNY SEDDON'S BOOT CRUSHES THE BROKEN EGGSHELL into smaller fragments as he clomps down the concrete steps, past the chalked graffiti, and swings along the walkway dodging the puddles. A clinging veil of drizzle is whipped in to flurries by the buffeting wind; already the sodium-yellow street lamps are lit, each globe encased in a husk of damp.

He's fairly slim yet solidly constructed, this lad Kenny, with slightly bulbous eyes, a full loose mouth and large raw hands on which the nails are nearly bitten to the moons. On the fingers of his left hand are tattooed the letters L.O.V.E. while on those of the right, H.A.T.E. He has a nervous habit of clenching and unclenching his right fist, an involuntary spasm of nervous energy, as though he were constantly about to hit somebody. Having been a manual worker since he left school, his arms, particularly the forearms, are out of proportion to the rest of his body: solid, heavy and with a blunt purposeless strength as if the power contained within them were impatient to be used up.

Taking a short cut across a worn corner of the empty flowerbeds he feels a slight catch in his throat at the thought of the menacing night ahead. Night-time frightens and excites him: the dark prowling streets are his natural habitat where he can escape the eyes of parents, bosses, the law, and all the other snooping, interfering busy-bodies. He's out of sight there, out of reach. The bastards can't touch you in the streets; they're afraid of the dark, of the unknown.

The chill air strikes into his chest and Kenny shivers once, a swift tremor down the back of his neck and across his shoulders. It makes his testicles curl up like little blind slugs. The dim blurred cubes of the Estate behind him, Kenny barges through a swing-door and into the Friday-night warmth, beery smell and stale smoke of the Weavers. In the tap-room Crabby, Arthur and Skush are playing darts in the corner underneath the single dusty bulb; a path has been worn through the linoleum.

Crabby has a gaping grin. His eyes are imbecilic brown, semi-glazed from the vacuum within. The tap-room regulars continue to play their games of dominoes and crib, oblivious to everything except sclerosis, cancer and avarice. The handlettered sign on the nicotine-coated wall says:

POSITIVELY
NO GAMES OF CHANCE
ALLOWED HERE

Elsewhere in the town on this Friday night the pubs are packing them in: a multitude of hands passing money over the bars, like a close-packed legion of Nazi salutes, reaching for slopping pints and slim-stemmed glasses containing whisky at evaporation point. While in the Weavers the smoke has become so thick you could cut it with a shovel. An old wreck in the alcove near the fireplace — a foreigner by his accent — carries on a monologue about the price of eggs, pronouncing his 'w's as 'v's and wice-wersa.

"Listen," says Crabby, "I vote we go to the Pendulum." His eyes are a-gleam. "I know this bird, fit as a butcher's dog. A right goer. Like a rattlesnake."

"Yeh," says Arthur. "We heard it."

"We heard it," says Kenny, swilling beer into his mouth. "It'd be like dipping it in a bill-paster's bucket." He doesn't like making quick decisions, particularly on a Friday night, because once you've decided where you're going it precludes the possibility of going anywhere else. Anyway he's got Something Lined Up for later on, so why go looking for it? A sudden pain in his left knee — an old footballing momento — makes his face twinge. Arthur is ripping up beermats, his long black oil-rimmed nails tearing absent-mindedly at the fibrous material.

Skush is the quiet one; he drinks his pint slow and calm and waits for the others to make up their minds. He's never been out with a girl, never had it (unless you can count his experience as a five-year-old behind the garages with Marlene Hiller, pulling down her fluffy blue knicks), and now and then he wonders if it's possible to get his end away without involving a female. That's what he'd like most: getting his end away without the acute pain and torture of having to approach a girl, talk to her, make easy conversation while all the time his lips are numb and his throat squeezed tight and dry. He has a couple of pills in his pocket that he's saving for later on.

They clatter down the narrow streets, echoes banging back and forth from wall to wall. A cat sneaks into the shadows. An empty milk bottle stands on a doorstep until Crabby kicks it into the gutter. The owner of the house opens the door and closes it again.

On Drake Street, merry with drink and laughing like drains, they cram into the Fusilier. The Irish landlord looks askance and pulls three pints without moving his eyes. Near the small platform with piano and drums a hen party is in riotous progress, a dozen girls telling dirty jokes and shrieking into their Cherry Bs and port-and-lemons. Kenny is attracted and disgusted by this behaviour; he reckons women should keep their gobs shut and not make a display of themselves—yet a gang of birds on the town is always game for a bit of the old how's-your-father. And if you don't buy a ticket you can't win the raffle, he thinks, standing above the circle of bright faces and attempting to make with the repartee.

"Ooo-ell," one of them says, all ringlets and sticky lips, "if it isn't Omar Sharif."

Kenny smiles; but he's holding himself inside. His eyes are like cold black marbles. Round and about people are grinning with their backs turned, but he knows they're thickheads and can take it.

He says, "Thank you Miss United Kingdom."

"Go home and send your dad," the eldest in the party, a woman of about twenty-seven, tells him. More shrieks and stricken laughter.

"You couldn't afford him on your pension." The old boot.

"Run along, sonny, and drink your Tizer."

Arthur is chatting up a girl with a pale round face and startling green eye-shadow, resting his forearms on the back of the chair and chewing gum in her ear. She looks as though she might be tempted, glancing up now and then at Arthur and giving him a small timid smile.

Crabby turns his back on the table and mutters to Kenny out of the corner of his mouth. "There's bugger-all here. We should have gone to the Pendulum. Least there's some decent music there." He has a fine faint scar on his jawline which shows through the soft adolescent stubble. "Come on, let's piss off."

"Hang about," Kenny says, watching Arthur and the girl: he wants to see what happens. At the same time he's trying to think of a remark he can toss over his shoulder at the hen party. Women in a group are all the same, they get cocky and smart and think they're being dead clever. But he wouldn't mind tackling the older one, taking her on Rochdale market after the pubs shut and giving her a good grope in the shadows; she has a big firm pair.

"You don't get many of them to a pound," he says to Crabby.

"You wouldn't get within sniffing distance."

"Who's bothered anyway; they're a load of old slags."

"What about the Pendulum?" Crabby whines. His face has a debauched pallor under the fluorescent lights. Not a single thought worth preserving has ever passed through that shaven skull. He left Holborn Street School in Brimrod when he was fifteen and started work in the stockroom at Asda Queens, which is an old defunct cotton mill in Castleton that's been converted into a giant supermarket. He was fired when they caught him with eleven packets of

Lyons Quick-Brew Tea and four bars (one partly eaten) of Galaxy chocolate stuffed into various pockets and down the inside of his boots. Whether it was because he had a passion for tea and chocolate was never satisfactorily explained. His next job was in the dispatch department of the Dexine Rubber Company, sending out parcels of ebonite washers to firms manufacturing washing-machines and refrigerators. He stuck it for three months and then didn't bother to come in one Monday morning. Since then he's worked intermittently in a garage, as a coalman, and on a building-site. At present he fixes television aerials to people's chimneys. Kenny knew him at school and their friendship was cemented when they played hookey and went on a joint shoplifting expedition to Woolworth's.

Kenny's heavy eyelids are drooping — partly the beer and partly the dull sluggish excitement rising in his throat. He stares insolently at the older woman and she wrinkles her nose as though at an unpleasant smell, sending the girls into fits of giggles.

"Past your bedtime, innit?" the woman says, the receptive captive audience making her rash and confident.

For a moment Kenny's face is contorted, and then he smiles slowly. The woman's handbag is underneath her chair, and accidentally on purpose he places the heel of his boot on the shiny black plastic and puts his full weight on it. There is a splintering crunch of plastic and glass.

"You bloody moron," the woman says. "What do you think you're doing?"

"What's the matter with you?" Kenny says, looking mildly surprised.

"You and your great clodhoppers."

"Is that your handbag? Daft place to leave it, under a chair."

"Paddy," the woman says, "throw this yobbo out."

"I'd like to see him fucking try."

"You bloody hooligan."

"Get stuffed."

"Paddy!"

Kenny suddenly wearies of this confrontation. Everybody in the pub is watching, but because he doesn't give a damn his hands are perfectly steady as he offers a packet of Number 6 to the other three. "Come on, let's drift." The four of them drink up and wander casually to the door, not meeting a single pair of eyes all the way.

On the corner of Drake Street by the Wellington Hotel they buy hamburgers from a young boy in a soiled apron who stands in the gutter with a strange contraption that resembles the mutation of a washing-machine on bicycle wheels. At this hour people are drifting aimlessly about from pub to pub. The town centre is awash with streetlight, everything pale yellow and slightly sickly-looking. Like being inside a fish tank filled with urine.

"What did your old lady say?" Arthur inquires of Kenny.

"What about?"

"Taking that bird home."

"What could she say?"

Skush laughs under his breath, embarrassed and envious.

Crabby brandishes his fist. "I bet you didn't have it away."

"I bet she's still a virgin."

"I bet my boot would fit into your gob."

"Smooth talker," Arthur says. They all laugh and start kicking at each other. A crush of women emerges from the Empire Bingo, vacuous expressions on pallid faces, the wafting odour of cheap perfume softly cloying in their nostrils on the cold dark air. The women scurry along in pairs, linking, their hard white hands clutching each other's sleeves and holding their handbags tight to their bodies.

The lads shoulder through them disdainfully. In actual fact Kenny—the others too—is afraid of these grim squat women with their set lips and stiff lacquered hair, yet won't admit it to themselves, let alone the others.

Kenny spies a girl he knows coming towards him. She works in the office of the engineering firm where Kenny drives a lathe all day. He think's she's called Sandra: longish blonde hair sweeping either side of a small, pretty, weak face: a pointed chin and almost no lips.

"Hello Sandra."

"Hello." She's like a child, standing there unflinchingly under their collective stare.

"Where yoff to?"

"Home."

"Yad enough?"

"She hasn't had any." Arthur.

A slow grimace sours Kenny's face. "Excuse my friend, he's got a spastic brain."

"Better than a spastic prick."

"See you," Sandra says, preparing to go.

"Hey," says Kenny, putting his arm round her. She has small bones and he can feel her tiny sharp shoulders through her coat. Not a bad little sparrow to make a nest with. He could show her a couple of things. She could show him two or three things. The beer has warmed his gut so that suddenly the night appears to him as a mysterious and almost a magical thing: his territory, his world in which daydreams become realities, and he experiences a sudden release as if from a strait-jacket. It's the simple combination of the beer and the dark.

"Isn't your name Kenny?"

"Yeh."

"Mr Tripp doesn't like you. He thinks you're a tearaway."

"What — Diarrhoea Features?"

"Is that what you call him?"

"Yeh. What the fuck does he know?"

"I don't know." A shrug. "That's what he said."

"That twat," Kenny says without any real malice, without expression. "Hey, where yoff to?" Sandra pauses in mid-stride and turns back. "Come and have a drink."

"I'll miss me bus."

"You what? It's only ten past ten."

"Me bus."

"Come on!"

She says something unintelligible and drifts away into the thinning crowd, small, a little lost, spidery legs in wedge shoes making her tread unnaturally, bent at the knees. Kenny clenches and unclenches his right fist. The sensation of the skin tightening over the knuckles is pleasurable but not consoling.

"Go on," he suddenly shouts. "It'd be like sticking it in a mouse's ear, anyway."

It isn't so much the shattered anticipation of having it away with her that angers him (he's got Something Lined Up) as the unpleasant taste of rejection, the humiliation of being dismissed with such tame indifference by a cheap little scrubber. He thinks of the girls in the Fusilier and their gaudy laughter, the ring of shrieking faces sharing a private joke as though its exclusiveness placed them in some special and privileged position when all the time they sweated and puked and excreted like everybody else, and what he wanted to do was smash that fake superiority and shake them and shake them until they saw sense and stopped acting like a bunch of overgrown schoolgirls creaming their knicks...

He belches and farts together; his senses are beginning to drift; a rubbery numbness is creeping into his face and hands. The screams and chatter and guffaws in the Flying Horse merge into a dull background roar and his eyes keep sliding off objects. He can't see Janice anywhere—though it is difficult to take in at a beery glance any individual face in the crowd pressing itself several deep to the bar. Crabby is acting the fool with a young bit who looks no older than thirteen. She has a couple of mates with her, all three weenies jiggling their bottoms in tight dresses and holding what appear to be outsize cigarettes in their chubby little paws. They puff at them tentatively as though they might explode at any moment, drawing the smoke shallowly into their throats and quickly exhaling through their nostrils. This place, with its carpets, colour TV and its hewn plastic beams overhead within touching distance, is the prime picking-up shop for the town's under-twenties. Indeed, most of them are under drinking-age, Kenny and three companions included. Since there's nothing much else to do, they drink.

The night is overwhelming Kenny. The sense of it is like an unexploded bomb ticking away quietly at the base of his brain: a thousand possibilities await him out there, none of which are within his power to realise. Through his semi-drunken stupor he perceives everything with a peculiar kind of clarity — sees, or rather feels in his gut, a bitter injustice. He realises, almost by instinct, that the game is rigged. It is like being slowly suffocated, crushed; he can't breathe, and wants to yell out at the top of his voice at the stupid senseless people in the bar who are drinking, smoking, babbling, shrieking, all to no purpose. Staring blearily around him, his head muffled in a haze of alcohol, he thinks: They deserve everything they get. They're parasites, the lot of them. They're neither use nor ornament to anybody. All they can do is guzzle and sup and act stupid. I wouldn't give them house-room. They deserve everything they get. Every fucking thing.

. . .

They walk towards the General Post Office, a square white building squatting opposite the Town Hall which looks like a shopsoiled birthday cake on which the icing has faded. A few lads they know are lolling in the Castleton bus-shelter, idly kicking at the panes of glass. This is a game of skill and chance where the trick is to kick the glass as hard as you can without it breaking. Eventually of course it does break, but in the meantime they innocently pretend to themselves that the intention is not to do any damage; then if the glass breaks it's its own fault. An old man and a courting couple are in the shelter, huddled into obscurity. Crabby tells Kenny that the Lake Greasers were down earlier on their bikes, a dozen of them roaring round town, obviously asking for it.

"We haven't been up there for a bit," Kenny says. "Do they still go to the Lake Cafe?" This is Hollingworth Lake, a local beauty spot, three miles outside Rochdale heading towards Yorkshire. There's nothing much there in the winter: a couple of restaurants, a cafe with trestle tables and rickety chairs, a corporation car park, and a tiny concrete basin where the naked masts of small yachts point at forty-five degrees to the sky.

A pane cracks and the lads stifle their laughter. The old man looks over his coat-collar and the courting couple huddle deeper in a passive embrace.

"Go on," one of the lads encourages Crabby.

"Do you think I daren't?"

"You daren't."

"*You* daren't."

"You're soft. Go on."

"Why, just because you tell me?"

"Because you bloody daren't."

"Who says?"

"I'm telling you."

"You're telling me?"

"Yeh."

"You?"

"Yeh."

"*You?*"

"Yeh. Go on."

"Oh fuck it," Kenny says, putting his foot through the glass. There should be a copper, or more probably two, floating about nearby, and there are. The lads retreat to the dark end of the shelter; the only trouble is, it's sealed off. They have two escape routes to go for, both at the top end of the shelter. One copper comes in each entrance, their helmets almost touching the roof. The lads wait, absolutely still, the blood pounding in their necks, their chests so full of air they can hardly breathe. One policeman moves past the old man and the courting couple: there's an iron rail running lengthways dividing the shelter in two and his body seems to fill the space between the rail and the glass panels. The other policeman waits by his entrance.

"Right," the advancing policeman says in an unnaturally steady voice.

"What do you want us for?" Crabby says in a voice shaking with bravado.

"Which one of you?" the policeman says. "Or I'll take the lot."

"Which one of us what?" Kenny says. He has slightly wet his trousers and he feels a dreadful excitement building up inside. His brain is churning and yet he's too preoccupied to pay it any attention. He thinks: Two steps nearer then right in the balls and over the top and up the Esplanade ... six of us scatter and they won't know which to chase and whoever they catch it won't be me.

"All right then, the lot of you," the policeman says, and in a voice low enough so that the old man and the courting couple can't hear: "You cunts."

He's not one of the younger constables, this one, he's a seasoned campaigner and as if by thought transference the lads realise that at least one of them — it could be two, even three — will get the chop this night and be hauled by the scruff to the shiny new police head-quarters which are no more than three minutes away even in a prone, semi-conscious, feet-in-the-gutter position. Kenny suddenly knows who the copper is: Sergeant S——, and simultaneously the Sergeant recognises him. He even smiles a little bit. Then he nods once, very quickly, to the other policeman (a young one) who takes out his pocket radio.

Arthur moves first, which Kenny is glad about, because the one who goes first always gets the worst of it. But Sergeant S—— lets him go and is still standing there, a big dark bulk between the rail and the glass-panelled wall. Two of the other lads try next and as they do Kenny goes in a blind headfirst rush at the young copper who is speaking on his pocket radio, catching him (for some reason Kenny can't understand) on the shoulder, feeling the rough scrape of thickish material against his face and smelling for an instant a clean, fresh smell of aftershave before he's out and free and running faster than you would suppose in his red leather boots across the two empty strips of tarmac, past the Town Hall and up the long flight of crooked steps into Broadfield Park. His heart is pounding as much with excitement as from the running and it's only when he reaches the top of the steps and stops to listen for pursuing foot-steps, that he realises how badly he needs to urinate. He does so, splashing it into the dark shrubbery in a panic of relief, biting the nails on his left hand while he listens to the silence which is some-how muffled by the roaring in his head. He then walks through the park, off the footpaths, treading lightly on the moist grass. They'll have alerted the Pandas but he knows the park well and also the several streets and alleys which adjoin it at right-angles. Suddenly he remembers that Sergeant S—— recognised him; if they're not waiting on the Estate now they'll have a car round tomorrow and he's in schtuck anyhow. Several plans form in his mind all togeth-er. He could say that it wasn't him, that they were mistaken, but they won't believe that. He could say he was in Heywood, missed the last bus and had to walk, but they won't believe that either. He could keep out of their way, but sooner or later they'll find him and pick him up. He could run away, hitch a lift on the motorway and go somewhere. Get right away from Rochdale, from Lancashire even, maybe down south somewhere, Birmingham or Coventry or somewhere. They'd never find him down there. He'd keep on the move. He could nick things and sell them to get money, moving from place to place. Kenny thinks of all the towns he's heard of, which to him are just names. He walks on the soft spongy grass in the middle of the park where it is very dark, the surrounding trees shading the yellow glare of the street lights. There must be somewhere he can go but he can't think of anywhere.

BEVVY

AS YOU DRIVE EAST ALONG THE M62 YOU SEE ON YOUR left-hand side, between interchanges 20 and 21, a large council estate of several hundred houses—Kirkholt—which is the biggest estate in Rochdale, with its own church, schools, shopping centre and social club. Running parallel with the motorway is Hilltop Drive, which you can look down on as you speed along the asphalt ribbon that follows the contours of the moors over into Yorkshire; and off Hilltop Drive is Rudyard Grove, a cul-de-sac comprising twenty houses or so. At number 18 lives Kenny's Auntie Doll. She's a plump, jovial woman with a beautiful set of pot teeth: a dazzling National Health smile that by its very brightness seems to hide a lifelong history of personal upsets and family crises. Auntie Doll is Kenny's mother's elder sister—sixteen years her elder, in fact, which puts her in the mid-fifties. Invariably she's smiling; this makes it difficult, if not impossible, to guess whether or not she's genuinely happy or yet again hiding one more miniature trauma to add to the catalogue of woes and calamities and misfortunes she has suffered since her marriage to Jimmy Mangan thirty-one years ago come April 3rd. If you don't have to live with him, Jimmy is a character; if you do, he's a drunkard. Although if drunkard is too strong a word for someone who at least manages to hold down a job now and again, then soak, inebriate and other such similar euphemisms make light of a situation in which every penny that finds its way into his pocket goes on drink before it has time to go anywhere else—rent, gas bill, holiday money, poor box. Doll has borne this state of affairs with forbearance and equanimity for so long that it's now become second nature to her; even more remarkable when you know that her father was afflicted with the same disease.

She escaped from a penny-pinching adolescence with a father who at weekends was transformed into a raging madman, to a married life in which bringing up three daughters and a son single-handed on the slops left over from the pub turned out to be a daily trial of strength. Yet, incredibly, she still smiles, and with her pot teeth she has something to smile with if not about.

Jimmy sits dozing in front of the fire, his feet bare, the flesh scorched a mottled pink. He grunts and slobbers in deep sunken sleep and comes sluggishly awake, eyes like peeled grapes, as Doll says, "Look who's here you drunken sod," and wrestles with his shoulder, the muscle run to fat. She even says this with a smile.

"Hey up," Kenny says, setting a pint bottle of Blue Bass in the hearth.

"Ken," Jimmy says, blinking foolishly, the eyes permanently out of focus. "Ken." He makes a slurping noise to take the taste away and then yawns cavernously. Kenny turns his face to the wall to avoid the sight as much as the smell. "Where's me tea?"

"You've had your tea. It's half-past eight."

"Get some glasses," Kenny says.

The man and the boy drink thirstily, the pale golden Bass sliding into their mouths. They talk about football, in which neither one is interested, while Doll moves to and fro in a parody of normal domestic activity. Although she spends, on average, an hour a day cleaning the house, the rooms never lose that appearance of shabbiness and untidiness which characterises certain working class homes. There are always crumbs on the table, newspapers on the floor and pieces of coal in the hearth, and the pattern on the wallpaper has been worn away in a faint streak where the backs of chairs have rubbed against it. When things get broken they stay broken until they're eventually thrown out, because Jimmy hasn't lifted a finger in the household for the last fifteen years.

"Dale went down again."

"Yeh."

"Did you go, then?"

"Yeh."

"Good game?"

"Not bad."

"Big crowd?"

"No."

"Who scored?"

Kenny doesn't know. He was groping Janice behind the Sandy Lane stand when they scored. He shifts awkwardly on the lumpy chair in his groin-tight trousers, trying to quell the memory. She's all right, Janice: a good laugh and a good grope, though he hasn't plonked it yet. He could plonk it right now though; if she was here, Christ could he plonk it.

"How's your mam?" Doll asks, smiling. (She would smile, Doll, were the heavens to erupt in chaos and the hydrogen bomb to fall on number 18 Rudyard Grove.)

Kenny can't be bothered to reply to this question. He up-ends the bottle into his glass and blinks once: that's the only answer she's going to get. He likes Doll but she's a woman and therefore of no account.

Jimmy puts the empty glass in the cracked hearth and asks what time is it? The pubs shut at half-past ten on Sundays which means less time to sleep off the afternoon binge before preparing for the final mind-blinding bevvy — all that separates him from the chilling black vacuum of Monday morning with its raw air and stiff greasy overalls scraping the skin and the upper deck choking on Park Drive. If he didn't have to work what a fine life Jimmy Mangan would have. As it is, he exists from pint to pint, hopeless, cheerful, indefatigably defeated: a human sponge with glassy eyes and a good body gone to pot.

"And where do you think you're going?" Doll asks. Jimmy is staggering about the kitchen looking for shoes and socks, tucking his collarless shirt into his trousers with one hand while supporting himself with the other. He cracks his toes on the leg of a chair and comes out with a mouthful. His previous good humour vanishes and he snarls and curses, pushing things out of his way, knocking stuff onto the floor. The house is a prison now; he gets into a blind rage and hates Doll and wants to harm her physically. She retreats into a corner, adopting a defensive posture (the smile gone for the moment) as Jimmy swings around the kitchen, colliding with the furniture. Once he attacked her with the bread knife and she retaliated by breaking his collarbone with a chair.

Kenny sits drinking his Bass, not unduly perturbed. He hasn't many illusions so far as people are concerned and very little they do surprises or alarms him. His own mother and father have a barney at least once a week, usually on a Friday night; it's the way folk live.

. . .

Jimmy is wonderful at the bar of the Dicken Green. The ale makes him quick-witted and hilarious, standing there unshaven in his collarless working shirt with a jacket draped across his shoulders. Andy, a mate of Kenny's, comes through the tables in the L-shaped tap-room. A wreath of smoke hugs the ceiling, slow streamers of it trickling down the walls. Although Kenny can't stand coloureds in general and Pakis at any price he doesn't mind Andy, who is West Indian.

"Hey up," says Kenny.

Jimmy Mangan stops. Then he stares. Then before tipping the pint into his mouth he says, "I always call a Spade a Spade", to the crowd clustering the bar, who respond appreciatively, digging each other in the ribs and laughing because they think Jimmy is genuinely funny and because if they don't he might throw something.

"Where you bin?" Kenny asks in an aside.

"Seven Stars."

"Back early."

"Dead."

"Seen Crabby?"

"No."

"Bin to town?"

"No."

"What you drinking?"

"Pint."

Kenny orders three pints and tells the barmaid she's got a tight little bum, like two hardboiled eggs in a navvy's hanky. She pulls her face in a kind of leering smile, undecided as to whether she should be flattered by the attentions of this strongly-built youth with the sloppy mouth and the tattooed knuckles. Kenny rests his meaty forearms on the bar and looks directly at her breasts.

"Do you want a photo?"

"What of?" Kenny responds, letting his jaw go slack and his mouth droop open in a dumb show of calculated insolence. His heavy-lidded eyes peruse the outlines of her black bra through her pale yellow blouse. He puts out his lower lip and continues to watch her sullenly as she lines up the pints in front of him.

"I dreamt about you last night."

"Did you?"

"No, you wouldn't let——"

A car screeches outside and everybody rushes to the doors to see a blue Ford Cortina sticking out of a lamp-post. There is glass all over Queensway and a man gets out with blood running down his face, which looks like black treacle in the anaemic light. Everybody watches to see whether he'll fall down or merely come into the pub to use the phone. Some people at the bus stop escort him across the road and sit him down on the pavement. The car doesn't burn. Kenny goes back to where Jimmy is halfway through somebody else's pint.

"Did he get the chop?" Jimmy asks between gulps. Kenny lights a Number 6 and shakes his head as he blows smoke out.

Andy says, "They're ringing for an ambulance."

"Bloody Spade," Jimmy says, standing there unsteadily at the slopping bar, his coat hanging half off his shoulders and the sleeve of his shirt wringing wet.

"It's all right now," Kenny says.

"What did he say?" Andy says. He's a biggish lad too, with a broad handsome face and a thick sensitive mouth. He has a razor-blade in his pocket with a strip of adhesive plaster down one side. Kenny grips the wrist of the hand that goes in the pocket in a gesture that is partly restraining, partly conciliatory.

"Go easy, he's had a skinful."

"Listen, dad——"

"It's okay," Kenny mouths.

"What's he on about?" Andy says.

"Nowt. He's bevvied."

"Spades." Jimmy emits a gust of air to signify what he thinks of Spades. The movement almost sends him reeling and he has to grab the bar, blinking with surprise, his head wobbling on springs.

"Now listen——"

"It's all right, he's me uncle."

"Well then," Andy says, "you'd better tell him," and staggers back, his hand nearly out of his pocket, as Jimmy slaps him on the shoulder in what is meant to be a friendly pat but is in actual fact a forcible blow.

"No fence, codger, me yold son, me yold son, me yold ..."

Jimmy tries to make his left hand (the right still clutching the bar) express what his tongue can't, waving it to and fro with a cigarette very nearly scorching his index finger. Andy looks at this beer-sodden wreck and decides it isn't worth it. But Jimmy Mangan has only to say 'Spades' one more time and he'll have a razor in his gullet.

"We'd better shoot off," Kenny says, giving Andy his pint.

"Th'all know me, th'all know me," Jimmy insists. "No fence to no man." He rifts deeply and the stench is putrescent. "Evry man his own, no matter what religion, colour, creed. Ask anybody here. *Any*body. Th'all know me. Ask them about Jim-iny Magnan— Manginum. He'll tell you, he'll tell you—this lad. Ken. Myyyyyyyyyy nefu. Neff-yoo. One of the bezt. He doesn't like Spades either."

"Oh fucking hell," Andy says.

There's going to be a barney, only Kenny doesn't like fighting with relations. Jimmy is a pain in the arse but when all's said and done he's a harmless old fart; and occasionally he slips Kenny half-a-bar which Kenny forgets to return and Jimmy simply forgets.

The gathering of old faithfuls round the bar looks on happily, awaiting with interest the next development. Jimmy is too bevvied to fight, of course, but he could put up a struggle that might be worth watching. Even seeing him fall on his arse would be good for laugh.

"Tell him, Ken; for fuck's sake," Andy says with a pained expression.

"Look ... cool it."

"Don't tell me—tell him!"

"He's old, he's past it, he's pissed."

"Then he should know better. I'm not going to take it, whether he's your uncle or not."

"He's just a useless old drunk."

"Tell him then. And make him shut up."

Kenny sighs; the world is on top of him. "Come on now, Jimmy, you've had enough. Doll will be waiting up for you."

"My neff-yoo."

"Aye, your nephew." He takes Jimmy by the arm and half-drags, half-carries him to the door. "I'll see him across the road," Kenny says to Andy. "Get us a pint in."

"Good neet, Jimmy!"

"Don't do owt I wouldn't do!"

"Watch yon bugger, he'll have you under a bus!"

"Don't knock any lamp-posts over on your way home!"

Kenny comes back a few minutes later and picks up his pint with the weariness of somebody returning from a Siberian labour camp. It's nearly time for last orders so he drinks the pint in one long gulping swallow and orders two more, wiping his mouth. Tomorrow it's work again: getting out of a warm bed and putting on overalls stiff with grease, shivering in the pre-dawn gloom of approaching winter as he walks through the Estate to catch the Deeplish bus on Milkstone Road. The walk is like the taste of iron in his mouth, with the Estate looking grey and unwashed in the dim glow of the wall-lights set in frosted globes. The bus is foul at this hour of the morning, thick with cigarette smoke from the close-packed seats, the smell of diesel oil dense in the nostrils, and the continual sound of hawking coughs and throat-clearings. There is hardly any talk as he sits there, cramped between the streaming window and somebody's arm holding the *Sun*, aware only that his bones feel like brittle sticks as the bus jolts over the humped canal bridge past the Kwik-Save supermarket on Well'ith Lane. Monday is always the worst morning of all, Tuesday is slightly better, and by Wednesday he is looking forward to the week-end.

Andy has made contact with the barmaid. She's thrown the towel over the pumps and stands with her hard round breasts resting on the bar. Kenny wasn't there to see the initial overtures and innuendos and he wonders for the umpteenth time how it is that Andy can never go wrong with the birds; he must have a great technique — unless it's simply because they fancy a bit of black for a change. He's talking to her in a low confidential voice, the two of them isolated amidst the noise and movement in a private cocoon of soft phrases and small intimacies.

The lights are flashing and the landlord calls, "All right, gentle-men, let's have you. Come along now. Your glasses please."

The barmaid looks straight at Andy and nods once. She mouths something with an exaggerated motion of her red lips, the lipstick faded at the corners, and goes to get her coat.

"What you doing?" Kenny asks.

"I'm okay." Andy drags on his cigarette and stubs it out in the ashtray.

"Have you trapped?"

"Could be," Andy says, never one to over-commit himself.

"Two's up."

"You must be joking."

"I'll push off."

"See you Ken."

"Yeh," Kenny says.

Queensway is humming with late-night traffic as he walks back to the Estate. He could do very badly with Janice tonight but it looks — as usual — as though he's going to have to settle for a hand gallop.

Rochdale Observer, 16 February 1974

PROBATION FOR YOUTH — A youth told police that as he and his companion were passing a grocer's shop in Oldham Road they saw a window was broken and decided to take goods. D—— A—— C——, aged 17, of Rhodes Crescent, Kirkholt, was put on probation for three years when he admitted stealing food valued at £7.04 from James Duckworth Ltd. Sergeant B Edmondson said two policemen on crime patrol saw C—— and another youth carrying objects under their coats. They ran, dropping a quantity of foodstuffs in the road. C—— told the court he had nothing to say.

WORK

THE WORKPLACE IS A LONG HIGH ROOM WITH DUSTY METAL beams overhead, piles of dust, metal shavings, waste, etc underfoot and the steady roar of oiled machinery. In winter in the late afternoons the sloping skylight above the metal beams reflects the shop floor as through huge inky-black mirrors: foreshortened people stride about hanging to the upside-down floor by their feet. At dinner time Kenny and some of the other men go to the chip shop on the corner for pie, chips and peas covered in lumpy curry sauce, and afterwards they kick a ball about in the cobbled street which separates Haigh's from Tomlinson's. Kenny is a nifty footballer, even in hobnailed boots; he puts more energy and enthusiasm into the midday kickabout than into anything that counts as work.

"You could have been a pro," Jack says. He's about thirty but could pass for forty-five. The hair is going and he carries a beer belly like a man hoisting a sack of potatoes.

"But for me knee."

"Cartilage?"

"Yeh. I was playing for the Dicken Green and it went."

"What did you play?"

"Inside-right."

Jack isn't so bad; at least you can talk to him But he's dead thick. On his first day at Haigh's he'd asked Kenny where the brewing-up place was and without batting an eyelid Kenny had pointed across to Tomlinson's and said with a straight face, "We get a brew over there," and Jack had trundled off into the other works looking for an urn of hot water. He'd brewed-up at Tomlinson's the best part of a week before somebody there thought his face looked unfamiliar and asked him what game he was on.

The hooter goes and they troop in through the sliding corrugated door. Immediately the whine of machinery starts up, the pulleys blur into motion and the leather belts slap about overhead. The foreman walks down the line, the pockets of his brown smock dark with grease. He stops at Kenny's lathe and shouts above the noise.

"Another lot when you've finished them."

"I haven't finished these yet."

"I can see that. Another lot when you have."

Kenny manufactures a sugary smile which he switches off in mid-beam, turning his back on the foreman.

"Don't be clever with me, laddie." Kenny pretends not to hear. The foreman taps him on the shoulder and jerks his thumb at the door. He shouts close to Kenny's ear, "Save yer yumour for when you get outside. Yer mates might appreciate it. I don't."

"You what?" Kenny says, screwing up his face.

For a moment they stare at one another, the loud machinery hammering the air, locked eye to eye with nothing passing between; just a hard blank empty stare. The foreman's tough now all right, Kenny thinks, but out on the dark prowling streets a quick boot in the bollocks and it'd be a different story. Personally he always went for the eyes; he got quite excited when he knew he'd got somebody in the eyes. They were soft, naked, vulnerable, the eyes, and as he thinks about this he has to swallow to contain his nervous response. For the next half-hour he dreams about the foreman's eyes and how he'd like to kick them in: him, Crabby, Andy and Arthur.

He could really get worked up thinking about what he'd done or wanted to do, even things that had happened a long time ago. One incident—when he was about nine or ten—never failed to excite him when he thought about it. He'd been walking home from school in the rain with another kid who must have been about seven. They walked down a dirt back-alley with deep muddy puddles everywhere and sharp broken housebricks poking above the surface. There was glass too; shattered bottles all over the place. Somehow or other (and he didn't know why) Kenny persuaded the kid to take his shoes and socks off. He took some persuading, and Kenny didn't use force because he wanted the climax of the incident to come as a complete surprise. The kid finally took them off: Kenny picked him up and carried him under the armpits to the centre of the largest puddle: he put him down on a couple of housebricks sticking out above the water and waded out again to watch what happened.

What happened, of course, was that the kid burst into tears. Kenny could still remember clearly the white, bare, wet feet on the broken housebricks; he could still remember how thrilling it had been to anticipate the kid having to walk through the dirty water in which bits of glass were embedded in the slime. What had thrilled him most of all, though, was the expression on the kid's face. He had one of those thin, pinched, snivelling kind of faces with a perpetual snotty nose, like two gobs of green candle-grease seeping from his nostrils. The face made Kenny sick; the scared, soft-as-shit expression on it made him want to throw up. He wanted the kid to suffer because of the expression on his face, and more than this, he wanted the kid to be hurt. Nothing would have pleased him more than to see those white smooth feet cut and bleeding. As it was the kid walked through the water, bawling his eyes out, and all his feet got were muddy. He did stumble once or twice, but nothing more. Thinking back on it Kenny was sorry he'd let the kid off so lightly. When he saw that the kid's feet weren't cut and bleeding he should have rushed up and pushed him full-length in the water. He was really sorry he hadn't done that.

On his way to the lavatory he passes Mr Tripp, a tall man with a beaked nose and the blackest of black hair slicked back and brillianteened to a high gloss. Mr Tripp worked in the office: he was always coming down with a bundle of papers in his dark hairy fist. The rumour was that he was knocking off the telephonist in the dinner-hour, a shy dumpy girl who sat hidden all day in a box of frosted glass.

"Official break ten past four," Mr Tripp says.

Kenny pauses, astounded, outside the entrance to the lavatory. He might have been lost for an answer, but he isn't.

"Who the fuck are you?"

"What did you say?"

"I said who the fuck are you?"

Mr Tripp is taller than Kenny; though he doesn't approach him. His eyes are black too, like his hair. Kenny recalls his nickname and his face cracks in a smile.

Mr Tripp grows tense. "I don't think it's funny."

"You would if you knew what I was laughing at."

Mr Tripp takes a deep steadying breath, is about to say something, hesitates, opens his mouth again and closes it. None of it needs to be said: it is clear as daylight the antipathy between them. All the stuff about the generation gap and the lack of respect youth has for its elders, and how the country is going to the dogs, and bring back birching and flogging, and they don't know they're born, and how a hard day's work would kill most of them, and a stint in the army would sort them out, and it wasn't the same in his day, etc etc etc.

Kenny knows all this and he delights in the fact of Mr Tripp's impotent rage. As for Mr Tripp he detests everything about Kenny, and particularly his physical appearance. The boy looks like a great dumb sullen imbecile, his shoulders bursting out of his shirt, the slack wet mouth and the slightly pop-eyed stare: for all the world like a baboon gazing vacantly through the bars of its cage. The baboon goes into the lavatory and enters the end cubicle with a copy of *Reveille*. It squats there for a while, reading and defecating, then quite deliberately, and with childish glee, shifts position so that the final turd drops on the floor. There's no toilet-paper, so the back page of *Reveille*, torn into strips, has to make do. Kenny grins at himself in the mirror: he has good teeth with only three fillings. He wets his forefinger under the tap and rubs it up and down against his front teeth. His toilet complete he goes back to his lathe.

The shop floor is close from the heat of the machines. With the afternoon now well advanced the day has gone from the skylight overhead: the strip-lighting along the metal framework throws a curtain of hard brightness onto everything below; each man has several shadows. It may be cold and dark outside but in here it's warm and cosy.

Kenny goes to the stores for a half-inch Wimet cutter and stops to talk with the storekeeper for ten minutes, an enormous man with close-cropped hair and a bull-neck, known to everybody in the works as Big John. His forearms are like hairy tattooed thighs and his paunch hangs in the shape of a peardrop from chest to groin. Big John is the fountain of dirty jokes at Haigh's, a man whose mind invents endless tales of sick depravity involving schoolgirls, nuns, spinsters, old ladies and all the members of the female office staff. He has broad, meaty hands padded with flesh and a face dominated by thick red lips. Legend said that Big John had a truly gigantic member — which Kenny didn't believe until one day he was taken into a small hot cubby-hole lined with blistering pipes behind the main boiler and witnessed the phenomenon with his own eyes. There was a magazine propped against the wall showing a young girl with bare breasts and pubic hair (this to give Big John an erection) and when the legendary member was fully extended twelve two-pence pieces were balanced along it and as a final, triumphant flourish, a half-pence piece placed on the very tip. It was a ritual that was repeated each time a new young apprentice came to work at Haigh's, so that Big John had the respect and envy of every lad there.

Kenny finishes the batch and humps the three skips of components to the checker's bench where a couple of middle-aged women sit listening to a transistor radio, their eyes downcast, their hands mechanically sorting through piles of polished components and stacking them like fat silver coins. He's heard rumours about these two old crones, in particular what they do to young apprentices, such as sticking their limp pricks inside a milk bottle and then getting one of the younger girls to lift her skirt so that the apprentice has an erection and finds himself trapped, having either to smash the bottle (a dangerous remedy) or tuck the bottle inside his trousers until the cause of his embarrassment has resumed its normal proportions and he can free himself. Kenny can't decide whether he's attracted or repelled by this — attracted, certainly, by the thought of a young girl willingly displaying her thighs but repelled at having himself exposed to the rapacious gaze of two disgusting old slags.

"Wasn't you we read about in the paper, was it?" one of them, Doris, says, her voice coarsened with shouting above the machinery.

"What?" Kenny says, standing there in a ragged shirt, his bare arms hanging at his side.

"Did you see that, Mo?"

"No?"

"In the *News of the World*. About them lads at that football match."

"Aye?"

"Ten of them attacked a young copper."

"Oh?"

"Broke his ribs and fractured his skull."

"Eeeeh."

"He's on the fatal list."

"No."

"Ten of them on to one."

"Shame."

"Wife and two young kiddies."

"Well."

"Wasn't you, was it?" Doris says, not looking up.

"Aye," says Kenny, "it was me all right. Duff a copper up every night, don't I?"

"Wouldn't put it past you," Doris says, not altogether joking. She has hairs on her chin.

"Have you finished that lot?" the foreman shouts at Kenny. Kenny stands looking at him. "What are you doing here, then?" the foreman says.

"Waiting for a bus."

"Ha-bloody-ha. Go on, there's another lot wanted for tonight." Kenny turns. "Hey." Kenny stops. "We've had a complaint about you."

"Me?"

"You."

"Who off?"

"Mr Tripp in the office. Says you were giving him cheek."

"Did he?" Kenny says, bored.

"Don't stir it round here, laddie. Just get on with the job; all right? We can do without——"

Kenny's face has suddenly gone stiff. His heart feels to be expanding like an oversized fist. He hates the foreman, he hates Doris and Mo, and above all he hates Mr Tripp. He pictures the boot going into the eyes. His right hand closes, opens, closes. The foreman registers none of this; his voice goes remorselessly on:

"We've had troublemakers here before but they've never lasted long. Just get on with the job. No need for any backchat, no call for it. If you want to give cheek wait till you get outside. You come here to do a job of work, that's all, nothing else. If you can't keep a civil tongue in your head then you'd be better off keeping it shut. You're not indispensable, you know. I can't weigh it up, you youngsters today, you think the world owes you a living. When I was a lad we buckled down and got on with the job, we had to, but not you lot today. No. Never satisfied, never content. If I'd cheeked anyone when I was your age I'd've been out. Out. No messing. Trouble is, there's no discipline any more, you're not kept in check like we were. Nothing clever, you know, in shooting your mouth off, anybody can do it, any silly twerp. Of course your generation never went in the army, did you? They'd have sorted you out all right, two years' square-bashing with a sar'major on your back all the time, that'd have knocked some sense into you. By the left. Five years I did, during the war, and it never did me any harm. *And* I was prepared to work when I came out, had to; but not you lot, not any more. You can't go two minutes without coming out with a mouthful, effing this and effing that. Causing trouble. I don't know what gets into you. I suppose it's your parents who're to blame, not checking you when you get stroppy. A good leathering when you were a kid wouldn't have gone amiss, but no, not today, they think the sun shines out of their little bleeders' aresoles. Anyway, think on, let's have less of it. Any jawing to be done and I'll do it. Right?" He puts his hand on Kenny's shoulder in a not unfriendly gesture and Kenny knocks it off.

"Wasting your time," Doris says. "Talk till you're blue in the face. They don't take a blind bit of notice even when you tell them."

"Well," the foreman says, "we'll see."

"I'm telling you," Doris says.

Kenny goes back to his lathe and puts the first component into the jaws of the chuck, tightening them up with the key. He presses the green button and the motor starts, and keeping his foot on the metal brake lever increases the power to give maximum revolutions. After a few minutes sparks can be seen flashing through the ventilation grille in the dark interior of the casing and smoke comes out in a thick blue cloud.

JANICE

KENNY STOPPED GOING TO THE CHAMBERS UNDERNEATH
Rochdale Town Hall when he was fifteen because it was—as he
described it—'baby soul'. It's one of the few places in town, pubs
apart, that caters for kids of twelve and upwards, and Kenny had
some good times there. It was at the Chambers that he first met
Janice: Andy had made a date with Janice's friend and this friend
had asked Andy if he had a mate to go with Janice, who at that time
was thirteen and a half. Kenny wasn't all that keen but he agreed
for Andy's sake, and the four of them used to meet at the Chambers
on Wednesday nights. It didn't last long, though, just two or three
dates, and after that they went their separate ways. She was a
scraggy, timid-looking creature who always had a wad of chewing-
gum in her cheek, and Kenny wasn't sorry to see her go. About
a year later, at the Seven Stars in Heywood, Kenny saw Janice
dancing on the floor and for a minute couldn't believe his eyes; she
wasn't any longer a sickly weenybopper; had in fact developed into
something he could almost fancy, and when she came off the floor
started chatting it up. In a lackadaisical fashion they started going
out together, both of them pretending that it wasn't a steady
relationship but more often that not happening to be in the same
place at the same time.

Kenny had to take some stick from his mates (Andy excepted)
who were all really desperate for girls but sublimated their yearn-
ing in beer, dirty jokes, piss-taking and rowdy behaviour. Kenny
didn't give a toss: he found that he liked Janice, enjoyed her company, and it was a challenge because she wouldn't let him have it
straight off. He reasoned that if it was that precious it might be
something special and worth getting hold of. (Like most men he

was attracted by goods that were openly on display but not for immediate sale.) Kenny met her mother too, an easy-going sort in her mid-thirties with a full high bosom and a ripe laugh that was all the riper after half a dozen Guinness. He couldn't figure out how mother and daughter could be so different, because Janice was essentially a quiet, almost shy person whereas her mother was larger than life and always seemed to have a fella in tow. She was generous as well and never seemed to be short of money even though she didn't appear to have a regular job. It occurred to Kenny that she might be on the game; however, he never said anything to Janice because it wasn't all that important. Janice and her mother lived in a private flat on Bury Road that was one of four above a row of new shops. There was some arrangement whereby the mother was in charge of the flats — caretaker or manageress or something — although Kenny never could fathom it out, even after Janice had explained it to him.

They started going to the match together, which at first was sacrilege to the others who stood with Kenny behind the goal at the Sandy Lane end. There had always been female hangers-on, of course, but they were anybody's. Taking an actual *girlfriend* to the match was definitely setting a precedent and took a bit of getting used to. Kenny never had, and didn't now, take much notice of other people's opinions; he really didn't give a monkey's; if they didn't like it they could stick it. Crabby made the usual remarks until Kenny told him to shut his hole. It wasn't Janice he was protecting, or rather, it wasn't Janice as a person: it was his property, and nobody took the piss out of Kenny's property.

Janice was still going to school around this time and had one more year to do before she left. In many ways she wasn't typical of her generation, who with hardly an exception were rabid Donny Osmond and/or David Cassidy fans. Janice preferred Tamla Motown, which is probably why she and Kenny hit it off in the first place. The Pendulum was where you went to listen to this kind of music, a gloomy basement with a low ceiling, a concrete floor and inadequate lighting that shared the premises with MSG (Manchester Sports Guild) Club on Lower Millgate just along from Victoria Station. Membership was 22½ pence, the beer was at pub prices and nobody bothered if you turned up in Wranglers, an old sweater and baseball boots. It was a dive in every sense of the word, a focal point for working-class kids from within a radius of ten miles of Manchester. In complete contrast to the Pendulum you had Time & Place, a disco in the basement of the next block, with its thickly carpeted stairs, flashing strobe lights, bouncers in tuxedos and, in the narrow street outside behind Manchester Cathedral, the ranks of Spitfires, MGBs, souped-up Minis and Volvos parked nonchalantly on the pavement. The girls who went there wore long evening dresses with cleavages that showed foreign tans, more often than not came from Prestwich, and their fathers had small businesses in the Ancoats district. The men who accompanied them were tall and slim; their chins were covered in Brut and their hair had been washed, cut and styled by Harvey and Rupert on Bridge Street.

To Kenny they might have been Martians. Their lives, their background, their upbringing, what they did for a job, and they themselves, were incomprehensible to him. They could have been a totally alien species for all he knew—and at the same time (it goes without saying) he despised them, partly through not understanding them and partly because they possessed worthless things like nice clothes, cars and self-assurance—worthless because he didn't believe they had really worked to obtain these things. But neither did he believe in work himself. It was a mug's game: senseless, futile and boring. A good job was a job that combined the maximum amount of money with the maximum amount of skiving. But neither did he desire a lot of money, nor the things that money could buy. It wasn't a case of opting out; it was a case of never having joined.

If looks were anything to go by, Janice could have done a lot better than Kenny. But of course looks, for a woman, are rarely anything to go by. Janice had first been attracted to him because he didn't seem to care about anybody or anything, her included. He wasn't bothered whether she liked him or didn't like him. The second thing that she found attracted her to him was that he made her laugh. He didn't crack jokes, he didn't go out of his way to be funny, and yet he made her laugh. He made outrageous statements with a perfectly straight pokerface so that she never knew whether he was being serious or taking the piss. (It's probable that Kenny didn't know either: he never did anything for calculated effect but blundered haphazardly through life, reacting blindly to people and circumstances in much the same way that a large, slack-jawed dog might inadvertantly wreck a living-room, breaking ornaments and spoiling the carpet.)

In the winter months of that year they used to see each other almost every night of the week, as well as going to the match on Saturdays and visiting each other's homes on Sunday afternoons. On some evenings they walked from the pub along Sandy Lane, the cemetery on their right-hand cold and silent behind its dirty millstone wall, a kind of thin blue haze in the air and people appearing suddenly before them muffled to the ears. They walked arm-in-arm, his thigh against her hip. Janice was proud of his bigness and liked the solid bulk of his arm around her shoulders; she was also frightened of him, of the unexpected, of not knowing him all that well. He had moods she didn't understand, for instance, which took her by surprise: a total lack of feeling—a vacancy—followed by a vicious spasm of anger which made him act with instinctive brutality, a mindless violence without any apparent justification.

The first time this happened, as they were walking, she experienced fear and excitement in the self-same instant. Then they were running from the scene of the incident, Kenny telling her to keep up, their chests hammering, and when they finally stopped, breathless, bursting into giggles because they were safe and together and the thought of the silly old man lying on the pavement with his false teeth in the gutter was irresistibly funny. Kenny hadn't intended to do it, the notion hadn't entered his head; but for the old man's dog yapping at their feet, and Kenny landing a kick up its hind-quarters, and the old man calling him a hooligan, and Kenny asking him to repeat it, and the old man being stupid enough to do so—none of it would have happened. Janice was glad somehow that it had happened. For one thing it made her feel closer to Kenny: it was a secret they shared together, and from now on they could refer to it in the company of others as 'that night near the cemetery' and nobody would be any the wiser. She liked the feeling that they, the two of them, were all alone in the world.

She remembered particularly, thinking back on it, the part when they were running hard up the blue misty road, Kenny's hand clutching hers and almost dragging her, the sound of their footsteps echoing from the high black wall, and the feeling—for the first time in her life—that she was a separate person who could now do as she pleased. She could choose her own way of life, decide for herself what she wanted to be; she was Janice Singleton; the thought beat in her head in time to the steps, and the feel of his hand in her hand made her aware that it had been Kenny who had been the first one to awaken this reponse. Then they were giggling and gasping in the darkness (it was down a dark rutted track where they finally stopped) and her head was pressing against his hard chest and his heart was thumping in her ear. She was in a wonderful dream. She was aware and proud of her small sprouting breasts and knew that this night was one she would remember always. A mawkish pop tune hummed in her mind … 'young love, first love, filled with true emotion …', and for the first time it actually meant something. This was young love, first love, this feel of his shirt scraping her cheek and his real body pressing against hers. She was in love with his strength, his big shoulders and warm solid arms.

Janice never again thought of the old man in any other connection than with the running, the breathlessness, the fear and excitement, and of Kenny's heart pounding close to her skull. And she thought about the secret they shared, and that feeling — very strong when they were running — of being closer to a human being than she had ever been before. And not only close, but one, indivisible, as though they were joined together and could never again be separated.

There was a postscript that proved to Janice the significance of the incident. The following Saturday morning her mother noticed an item in the *Rochdale Observer* about an old man who had been beaten up: she remarked on it because Sandy Lane was only a few minutes away down Bury Road, adjoining the cemetery. Janice listened with a bland expression, controlling a little smile which kept tugging at the corners of her mouth. It might have been a coincidence that her mother should have spotted this particular news item but Janice didn't think so. No, it meant that something had conspired to set her and Kenny apart from everyone else. The secret they shared was now even more *their* secret because what had taken place was common knowledge and yet only the two of them, of all the people in the world, knew the full truth. Sitting at the kitchen table watching her mother — still with the vestiges of last night's make-up on her face and her blonde hair uncombed — reading from the paper, Janice experienced a warm enveloping glow; her breathing became loose and she suddenly felt that she had to go to the toilet. And she would be seeing him again soon, that very afternoon at the match. A record came on the radio, 'young love, first love, filled with true emotion...' and it was as if her life, endlessly circular, had at last assumed a pattern, and all at once it came to her that she was a young woman growing up: that her mother sitting opposite her was, after all, only her mother.

Kenny's world became the real world for Janice. It dazzled her, intrigued her, scared her, thrilled her. Whereas before she had lived a kind of half-life, literally half-alive, now it became a strange adventure, dark with mystery. She couldn't express it in words... it was something she felt... something her body responded to which she herself didn't properly understand. School became a shadowy interlude through which she drifted in a dream-like state thinking about the night before or the night ahead. Marjorie, Janice's best friend, knew about Kenny and didn't think much of him. In her opinion he was a great lummox. Neither did she like it when Janice stopped going to the youth club on Thursday nights and even less when they ceased to visit each other's homes and play records while they discussed boys, make-up and popstars. As for Janice's mother, she noticed very little anyway. Maybe Janice wasn't in the flat as much as she used to be, and when she was seemed to spend most of the time in her room listening to soul records, but apart from that it didn't strike her that there was anything markedly different in her daughter's behaviour. Even when Janice started going away every other Saturday to places like Grimsby and Plymouth and Wrexham she took it for granted that this was a natural stage in the development of a fourteen-year-old girl.

Perhaps if Janice had had the influence of a father (who had died when she was three) she wouldn't have been allowed to roam where and as she pleased. Questions might have been asked, rules imposed, and a stricter watch kept on the company she sought. However, this is hypothetical: the fact was that never at any time was Janice asked to account for her movements, whom she met and what took place. Mr Casson, her teacher, once became concerned about her welfare and he might have mentioned it at the end-of-term Open Day. But Mrs Singleton hadn't bothered to turn up; consequently Mr Casson lost interest too.

One thing that might have made her sit up and take notice: if Janice had become pregnant, but as this possibility was unthinkable it was simply never thought of. Despite being an avid reader of the *News of the World* Janice's mother never once entertained the notion that a fate worse than death could ever befall her Janice.

CHORLEY

ONE SATURDAY NIGHT A GANG OF THEM MET OUTSIDE THE ABC cinema and couldn't decide where to go. They clustered round the brightly-lit entrance keeping out of the slanting rain, jostling one another and making rude remarks about the film that was advertised in the illuminated panel: *The Four Dimensions of Greta*. Inside, in the warmth behind the glass doors, the cashier (an old dear with a hearing-aid) exchanged outraged glances with the woman selling sweets, cigarettes and Butterkist from her cubbyhole barricaded with confectionery.

Crabby voted for the Pendulum but as usual was shouted down. Skush said, "What about the White House?"—a pub right on top of the moors a few yards from the Lancashire-Yorkshire border. Everybody jeered, "What about the White House?" and Skush turned his back, going red, and continued looking at Greta. He felt dizzy from the pills he had been taking, which so far that evening hadn't had time to produce the desired effect; he needed a couple of pints to really get them working in his head. What he really needed was a girl. What wouldn't he have given for a girl.

After a lot of pushing, laughing, falling about and futile discussion somebody came up with a plan of action: get the diesel to Manchester Victoria and buy a ticket for the next train scheduled to leave, no matter where it was going.

"We could end up in bloody Brighton!" Arthur said, excited at the idea.

"They don't go to Brighton from Victoria," Kenny said, and twisting his mouth to make the word sound even more scathing: "Twat."

"They could," Arthur said, sticking his chin out. "They could. All the lines join up so you could get to Brighton from Victoria. Nothing to stop you."

"Nothing to stop you except they don't bloody go from Victoria."

"I didn't say they *did*. I said they *could*. Could!"

"You bloody well said they did."

"I said they could."

"*Did*, you said."

"Could."

Crabby said, "We followed the Dale to Brighton."

"You didn't go on the train though," Arthur said, behind him on the stairs leading to the upper deck of the bus. There were seven of them and they each took a seat to themselves.

"I didn't say owt about a train," Crabby snarled.

"You went on the coach."

"I know we went on the coach."

"Ellen Smith's."

"Yelloway," Crabby said.

"Was it buggery Yelloway—Yelloway don't go to Brighton."

"How do you know when you weren't there?"

"Yelloway don't go to Brighton."

"How do you know when you weren't there?"

"I'm telling you."

"How do you know when you weren't there?"

"It was Ellen Smith's."

"How do you know when…"

This conversation didn't slacken off and finally tail away until they were on the diesel rattling over the points to Manchester Victoria. It was early for a Saturday night and there weren't many in the long rocking compartment: just the odd bird dressed to kill who had a boy-friend to meet under the station clock, and the occasional middle-aged couple sitting huddled together in hats, scarves and heavy clothes. Kenny took out the stick of indelible red marker and wrote his name on the back of the seat in scrawling capitals, adding, 'ASHFIELD RULE OK'.

"Give us it," Crabby said, leaning across the aisle.

"Piss off, lavatory face." Kenny jabbed at him and left a red mark on Crabby's chin. The others rolled about shrieking.

Andy said quietly, "Wherever we go let's find some birds."

"Yeh, let's get some birds," Skush said. His face was very pale and his watery eyes were staring out of his head. The pupils had shrunk to black dots, the proverbial pissholes in snow.

Fester, a short, very broad lad with a hanging gut from drinking too much ale, and enormous square hands like a robot's, took a metal spike out of his pocket (a pulley spindle specially sharpened at work) and pricked his name in the plastic covering; then for a full-stop pushed the spike clean through the seat where it struck Arthur in the back. It made a hole in his best jacket. There was a commotion, some fist-waving and threatening half-blows, but Arthur wasn't stupid enough to tangle seriously with Fester, who would have broken his spine in three places and wiped the floor, walls and ceiling with the remains.

Because he wasn't going to be outdone and because he liked the limelight Kenny stood on the seat and wrote all the dirty four-letter words he knew on the curved panels overhead, the rest of them shouting encouragement and trying to kick his legs from under him.

Andy, the coloured boy, sat with Skush, not taking any part in the general hilarity and merry-making but biding his time and saving his energy for the birds. He had already shafted three that week and badly needed another one tonight—not as badly as Skush, who had masturbated so much recently that he kept glancing fearfully at the palms of his hands as though expecting to see tufts of hair sprouting. Of course he no longer believed that it sent

[51]

you blind, but he couldn't overcome the feeling that it was unhealthy and not at all good for you; there was a rumour that it caused mental illness and even leukaemia. Now that the amphetamines had begun to take hold he was experiencing the curious sensation of being stimulated and depressed at one and the same time. His mouth was dry and his stomach felt hollow; he was alert and yet relaxed, calm and yet excited. He could handle a girl now, he knew he could, no doubt about it: just let him get to grips and he'd sweep her off her feet. He imagined a tall slim cool blonde with nicely-shaped knockers—like that one in Pan's People— who he could trust himself with and who wouldn't make fun of him. An understanding girl, that's what he needed, an understanding girl who was a good fuck. He looked down and realised that he had a respectable erection straining at the zip of his jeans.

Just then the ticket-collector came swaying towards them down the central aisle, steadying himself on the backs of seats with alternate hands, and the seven of them ceased their various activities to gawp at him, their faces gone stiff and sullen as if challenging him to check them or to make a remark. As he went by Kenny farted, a tight dry one and obviously difficult to produce. Crabby choked with laughter and finally managed to say in a strangulated voice:

"The Phantom Arse strikes again."

"Jesus Ker-ist!" Fester said, who happened to be sitting next to Kenny, wafting the air with his robot's hands and hanging his chin over the edge of the seat in front and pretending to spew.

"Good arse," Kenny said with a satisfied smirk.

"What've yad for your tea—black peas?"

"Sprouts," Kenny said, and became aware that he had strained so hard that a small amount of matter had been released with the wind: he had shit himself.

At Victoria they raced each other to the barrier and leapt shouting—like wild animals suddenly released—across the main concourse and through the people to the A-G ticket office, which was the first one they came to. The man behind the double glass looked at them down his nose, and in reply to Kenny's question said, "Chorley."

"Who the fuck wants to go to fucking Chorley?" Crabby shouted.

"Fucking Chorley cakes."

"Chorley, fuck me."

"Where's fucking Chorley?"

Fester's friend Pete (known as Shortarse because he was the smallest in the gang and who, for this reason, could always rely on Fester's protection) said, "We might as well go to Chorley as any-where. Better than being stuck here all night."

"Yeh, let's go," Andy said, groping for money.

They all bought tickets and trooped off to the platform to await the 8.17 to Chorley. It was a diesel, and nearly empty. On the journey they passed the time by telling dirty jokes, writing on the mirror in the lavatory, unscrewing the toilet seat and throwing it through the window, and calling obscenely to two young girls with a poodle who sat petrified at the far end of the coach. Kenny was all for approaching them (and would have done) had Andy not restrained him: there were several people on the train and they might have objected. In fact one of them did have words with the ticket-collector when he came round but by that time the train was pulling into Chorley station and the lads, shouting abuse, disem-barked. The ticket-collector put his head through the window to say something and at least three of them spat at him.

Chorley was deader than a doornail. It was still raining and the colours of the traffic-lights were smeared on the wet tarmacadam. They steered clear of the posh-looking places — the ones with full car parks and table-lamps lighting net curtains in a rosy glow — and sought out the small corner pubs down backstreets with *Snug* etched on their opaque windows and tap-rooms thick with pipesmoke and public bars in which cackling women with red lips and wrinkled stockings stood shoulder-to-shoulder with the men drinking cream stout in thirsty gulps. The lads crammed through swing doors with brass fingerplates into a long narrow bar with room enough for only a single line of wrought-iron tables stationed against the wall: between the tables and the drinkers standing at the bar on the worn strip of linoleum there was barely enough space to get by: it was one of the few pubs still remaining that had somehow resisted the encroachment of fitted carpets, Musak, and chicken-in-the-basket. And tonight, of all nights, it was a pub with no beer.

Kenny and the others couldn't believe it. They ordered seven pints of keg bitter and gazed at the landlord in bewilderment when he told them the bad news. It appeared that the brewery had missed a delivery and all he could offer them was pale ale, stout, and lager in bottles.

"Jesus Christ," Fester said. "A pub with no ale."

They tanked up on Blue Bass and Newcastle Brown, loitering in an untidy group, obviously set apart from the regulars. At least there was a juke-box (a miniature one fastened to the wall) but it was mostly top thirty crap with not a single soul record and hardly any Tamla Motown.

"Chaaawley," Arthur said in a funeral voice.

"A right dead hole."

"No deader than Rochdale," Shortarse said.

"Come off it."

Skush said, "Let's get where there's some birds." His voice was slurred and he couldn't focus his eyes properly. Kenny said:

"Have you any left?"

Skush looked at him stupidly. "What?"

"Bombers."

"What for?"

"Why do you think what for? Give us some."

"I've only got two."

"Give us one then."

Andy was feeling randy and suggested they move on to find a better place. Fester agreed; not for the sake of trapping off but because he wanted a pint of draught beer instead of the bottled muck they were drinking. On a good night he could shift ten pints and had been known to sink fourteen. Kenny prided himself that he could keep up with Fester—and he could—but he was usually sick afterwards, especially when they rounded the night off with beef pudding and peas and a double portion of chips, bread, butter and tea.

He secretly believed, too, that he could beat Fester in a fight. He had it all worked out: that flabby gut was a prime target for the boot followed by a knee under the chin as he came down gasping, then a double-fist on the back of the neck and a final boot in the cobblers to finish things off. He wouldn't go for Fester's little, piggy eyes; no—the gut, the neck, the groin.

"Are we going or are we not?" Fester asked irritably.

"Chaaawley," Arthur said again, doing his best to establish it as a catchphrase.

"Well?" Fester said, beginning to get on Kenny's wick.

"Yeh, come on," Shortarse said, backing up his mate.

Kenny wasn't going to be hurried by anybody, least of all by Fester. "Hang about," he said, "let's have another," wiping his mouth and taking out a pound note.

"For fuck's sake—"

"You go if you want to."

"We're all going," Arthur said.

"Come on then," Crabby said.

"Who wants another?" Kenny offered, moving to the bar. He was the tallest of them all, and the broadest next to Fester, who was broad but fat with it.

"Me," Andy said, who really wanted to move on but in the event of conflict always sided with Kenny. They stuck close together these two, an unlikely alliance considering that Kenny hated foreigners, and in particular Spades, Pakis and nig-nogs. One reason why he disliked them so much was the horrible stink of their cooking which seeped out of Number 468, two doors away from where he lived, and whose heavy sickly odour stuck in his nostrils every time he passed by. If they'd eat that stuff they'd eat shit.

"I'll have a Newcastle," Skush said, rapidly losing his sense of time and space. He felt peaceful and at one with the world, despite the shrill buzzing in his ears, and was content to drift along in a muffled cocoon of blithe indifference. He knew there was a girl waiting for him somewhere ... somewhere there was a girl waiting for him ... somewhere ...

Fester capitulated with bad grace. Kenny bought another round and they stood drinking in temporary silence, Fester throwing it back in three swallows. There was an exodus to the lavatory where they stood in line at the stones, having to relieve themselves in two shifts. On the contraceptive dispenser it said:

Approved to British Standard BS 3704

And underneath in felt-tip someone had written:

SO WAS THE TITANIC

It took Crabby several moments to get the point; when he did he laughed hoarsely, splashing urine over his shoes. The others laughed too, and it dissipated the ugly spite that had begun to erode the evening.

Chorley appeared to consist of nothing but a main road — the A6 — with several dark streets leading off it at right-angles. There was a cinema, a couple of Chinese restaurants, a coffee bar (closed), some shops and department stores at the junction where the traffic-lights flashed, and, so it seemed, more than its share of illuminated signs giving directions to Manchester, Bolton, Preston, Southport and the M6.

Kenny thought it a real dumb-hick town. Anybody who lived here must be dead thick. For some reason it annoyed him to think of people actually being stupid enough to stay here, work here, breed here, die here. Probably they saw nothing wrong with it; probably the kids who lived here reckoned it was an OK place. They wouldn't know any better. He came from a big town where everybody knew the score — but here, Chorley! — for Christ's sake, it didn't even have a league football team. They probably thought of themselves as smooth townies and yet they were nothing, washouts, zeroes. He became restless with the need to show them just how pathetic they really were, how this hole in the middle of nowhere didn't rate when compared with a Big Town.

"What a dump," Crabby moaned.

"Chaawley," Arthur had to say.

They cruised around looking for signs of life and had to admit, eventually, that they'd been lumbered. Or rather they'd lumbered themselves. By this time, however, they were well on the way to becoming kalied and so it didn't really matter where they were. There were pubs, and pubs sold beer, and beer got you slatted, and getting slatted was what Saturday night was all about.

In the fourth or fifth pub things started to get nasty. Of course they were always on the lookout for trouble — at the back of their minds seeking it, ferreting it out — but this came out of the blue: when a bloke with long greasy hair and a leather jacket with studs passed a remark about Andy. Andy confronted the lad who had made the remark but Kenny stepped between them. He had only been waiting for the opportunity, and now his patience was rewarded.

[57]

There was the usual terse dialogue spoken in an undertone consisting of 'what did you say?' and 'I was talking to him,' and 'what's it to you?' and 'if you want to pick a fight pick it with me', and 'don't come it', and 'none of your business', and 'don't get smart with me', and 'say that one more time', and 'I wasn't talking to you', and 'when you insult him you insult me', and 'keep your nose out of it', and 'let's see if you're as tough as your talk' and 'who do you think you're pushing?' and 'let's have you outside', and 'you and whose army?', and in no time at all a space has cleared around them and they are alone in a circle and the rest of the pub has gone quiet and the barmaid has run through to the tap-room to fetch the landlord.

Kenny and the lad with the greasy hair stare at each other, their eyes inches apart, pushing the other in the chest, at first gently and then with increasing force. On the fringe of the clearing the others stand shoulder to shoulder facing their opposite numbers across the worn carpet, several of them slipping their hands casually into their pockets. It has the makings of a right old barney.

"Outside," the landlord says crisply, grasping their elbows and pushing them towards the door. Kenny and the lad with greasy hair half-resist, still staring hard at each other, still murmuring threats under their breaths, being propelled reluctantly to the cold outer air and the slick-wet pavement and the lights gleaming through the haze of drizzle.

Fester closes in behind Kenny's back; Kenny's eyes don't betray a flicker as the transfer of the sharpened spindle takes place from hand to hand. He already has the broken half of a hacksaw blade in the back pocket of his Levis but he's not averse to consolidating his armoury. Also he has the boots with the reinforced toecaps and the chunky steel washers that fit snugly on to the fingers of his right hand. His shoulder bangs against the door, there's a glint of reflection from the massed bottles behind the bar, a shaft of cold air touches his legs, the door-hinges creak, and the two of them are thrust into outer darkness.

The other's eyes are hidden in shadow but Kenny can remember them: blue slits beneath eyebrows that bridge the nose and meet in the middle: a naked animal hatred coming at him through the holes in the skull. Kenny slips his fingers through the washers; the spindle is partly concealed behind his back in the folds of his jacket. They tentatively circle round like two dogs sniffing each other before a fight.

"You called my mate a nigger," Kenny says. It is important not to let the cause of the dispute be forgotten. There has to be a reason; it must be spelled out and made to bear the weight of their mutual hatred. It must generate anger.

"I said it to him, not you."

"Now you've got me."

"What's up, is he chicken?"

"You've got me," Kenny repeats. "So you'll never know, will you?"

"Thinks he's a tough nut," calls one of the lad's mates.

"You're next," Kenny says.

"Have him, Neil."

"I'll fucking have him," Neil says.

"Come on then," Kenny goads him. "Fucking come on then."

"Right."

"Right then."

"They're here," a woman's voice says, and quick as magic a Panda car is at the kerb and three policemen are thrusting through the crowd, pushing bodies aside and reaching out. Kenny hits the lad with the greasy hair in the face with the row of washers, and runs. His collar is grabbed and he lashes out blindly with his boot, meeting no resistance. A blow from what seems a sledge-hammer lands on his ear and he feels himself going down, off-balance,

failing sideways, the hand still holding his collar. He's on the pavement amongst a lot of legs, squirming, and goes on all-fours
through them, somebody or something heavy landing on his back;
then off his knees and on to his feet and almost running into the
wall before finding his bearings and clomping full-pelt towards the
main road.

. . .

"You could have taken him," said Fester, propping his feet on the
seat opposite. For the sake of expediency they had decided to catch
the first train back to Manchester.

"I could have taken him but for the rozzers," Kenny said. "He
was thick as pigshit."

"You got him a good one," Arthur said, grinning, showing the
gaps in his teeth.

"Who?"

"The greaser."

"Yeh." Kenny put his hand to his left ear, which felt as though it
was encased in rubber. And so tender he could hardly bear to touch
it. "I could have taken that fucking copper as well," he said intensely.

"He was a big bastard," Crabby said. "Broad."

"On his own I could have taken him."

"What a dump though," Crabby said, wiping the condensation off the window and trying to look out at the dark rushing
countryside.

"Chaaawley," Arthur said.

"What was the name of that place?"

"What?"

"That pub."

"Dunno."

"Royal Oak or summat," Shortarse said.

"No, that was the big place we passed. Didn't go in."

Fester raised himself off the seat and released a long, slow, full-bodied fart, his eyes closed and his lips compressed in a small beatific smile. The ensuing laughter was mingled with complaints and obscene abuse. Then Arthur let one go — a rasper — and they were all at it, and soon it was a contest, the idea being to see who could release the most in a given period. After the first round, Crabby, Fester, Shortarse and Kenny were leading, all managing to produce ten or more, and the others dropped out. In the second round Crabby's energy and wind failed him and he could barely achieve three, and pathetic squeaks they were; Fester started well but fizzled out towards the end of the thirty-second period, and so it was up to Kenny and Shortarse to compete against each other in the final round to decide who deserved the title of 'King Arse'. Arthur announced the start of the thirty seconds and the chant began as the two finalists twisted and strained and contorted themselves to extract the maximum emissions from the dwindling supply.

"... seven ... eight ... nine ... ten ... eleven ..."

It was neck and neck, fart for fart, and the total rose to fifteen ... sixteen ... seventeen ... where it stopped in apparent stalemate, the two contestants bending and doubling-up in a frantic effort to produce the winner. With seven seconds to go Shortarse managed yet one more.

"Eighteen!" went the chant.

His face nearly blue, Kenny equalised, knowing his underpants were caked but refusing to be beaten. Arthur counted off the remaining seconds. Shortarse was done for, and it looked as if the contest would result in a dead-heat, until with a last desperate contortion Kenny released a low-pitched bubbling sound which was generally acknowledged to be legitimate and allowable.

"Nineteen!"

Kenny flopped back on to the seat, triumphant but physically uncomfortable. The other passengers in the coach sat facing the front, their faces expressionless, their feet positioned carefully together so that they wouldn't obtrude into the aisle.

JEALOUSY MOTIVE
OF 'CLOCKWORK
ORANGE' ATTACK

A TEENAGE JEALOUSY led to a Rochdale schoolboy being lured to spare ground where he was beaten with chains and hit on the head by a bottle, magistrates heard yesterday.

Two boys, both aged fifteen, were put under supervision for two years by Rochdale Juvenile Court, and a third boy, also fifteen, was remanded to the care of the local authority for twenty-one days until he can be placed in a remand home.

The boy's mother told magistrates his behaviour at home was terrible.

She added: "He thinks nothing of hitting me or the other children. I can't cope with him any more.

"I have an awful time when he is in the house and I am glad when he is out. He has also hit his grandma who is an old woman."

The father of one boy said he had not noticed the vicious streak in his son before, and the father of the other boy said he could not understand this "Clockwork Orange-type of thing".

All three boys admitted wounding a boy, who, said Inspector Frank Jones, prosecuting, had left home with a friend to go to a dance.

They were met from the bus by the three youths who chatted with them.

Suddenly, the three boys pulled out metal chains and started to hit the boy on the head and body.

He tried to run away but one of the boys picked up a glass bottle and hurled it at his bead. He was wounded by the bottle which broke on impact.

His friend tried to intervene and he was also attacked with the chains.

One of the attackers told police that the boy they had first attacked had been going out with a girl his friend wanted to go out with. The attack had been planned.

BRASS

KENNY KNEW THE OLD MAN WOULD HALF-MURDER HIM IF he found out he'd been given the push from Haigh's. It was the third job in eleven months Kenny had been fired from: he had to keep up the pretence of working there until he found somewhere else—somewhere with as much if not more money than he'd been getting at Haigh's—and only then would he dare to break the news. The old man went berserk whenever Kenny was out of a job and made life hell on earth. But there wouldn't be much point in pretending if he couldn't give the old lady the usual sum on a Friday night, laying down the crisp oncers on the kitchen table; at least they didn't ask to see his wage-packet any more.

Kenny lay amidst the crumpled sheets and the torn-up wrappers of a Bounty bar and a Walnut Whip, staring blankly at the ceiling and biting his nails. The top pane of the window was open and the faint aroma of curry and spices wafted in from the landing above. Where was he to get the money? He thought of calling round to see Jack in the dinner-hour and touching him for a few quid, but even as the idea took shape he knew it was useless. Jack was a married man with kids and a mortgage and was scraping to make ends meet as it was. There had been occasions in the past, getting towards the end of the week, when Kenny had slipped Jack half-a-bar. That didn't leave many possibilities. His mates rarely had anything left themselves after beer and fags and a few games of crib, and even if they had he couldn't see them being generous enough to have a whip-round for his benefit. The only people who might be willing to help him out (and who could be trusted to keep their mouths shut) were Jimmy and Doll. There again, Kenny realised, they weren't exactly rolling in it. Together they must have been earning a fair screw, but no sooner was it in his pocket than Jimmy was handing it over to the landlord of the Dicken Green, propping up the bar seven nights a week. Now maybe if Doll had managed to put some by — wakes money, perhaps, or for some new clothes — she might be able to lend him, say, a tenner, which would be enough to see him through another seven days, and during that time he could get fixed up somewhere else. Jobs weren't plentiful but then Kenny wasn't fussy: if they paid twelve or over he'd grab their hand off.

As for Haigh's, he knew who was to blame for getting him the sack. Diarrhoea Features. The foreman would have reported the machine breaking down but it was that bastard Tripp who would have had words with the works manager and somehow or other put the blame on Kenny. Christ, a motor can burn out at any time, there's no telling when it might happen. Kenny felt a bitter injustice at his dismissal; they had conspired to get rid of him, Tripp, the foreman, the works manager, and probably even Doris and Mo. He didn't trust any of them, never had. All along he had sensed their animosity, a desire to do him down. He almost felt sorry for himself, as a child might when told by its friends that it can't join in their game, but the self-pity was submerged in still deeper and unfathomable hatred. He plotted with himself how he could get even, worked out elaborate plans that ranged from waiting for Tripp one dark and moonless night in an alley to sneaking into the place one Sunday and burning it down. In his mind he saw the flames, and Tripp was in them, trapped under a fallen beam, screaming, his black hair singed to the bone.

It had been the same wherever he had worked. Before long they found an excuse — or rather invented an excuse — to get rid of him. Kenny knew the reason: it was because he was young and they were old. They were past it, over the hill, their own lives finished and empty and done with, while his was just beginning. They couldn't bear to think that he had the world at his feet and that their world was dying. Kenny knew this for a certainty: for the simple reason that he knew the score and they were dead thick.

But the problem of the money remained. He had to get some, if only enough to last the week, otherwise the old man would go spare. Brian was like a mate to him at times — they had been out drinking together, for instance — but if one thing was guaranteed to drive him wild it was Kenny being jobless. In one respect this was hard to understand because as a young man himself Brian had had more jobs than Kenny had had hot dinners. Now he worked, bowed down by the responsibility of a wife, two kids, a home to keep up, and the hire-purchase payments on the living-room carpet, the cooker, and the new stereo radiogram with its smooth teak finish that he never bothered to listen to. His frivolous days were behind him; respectability was here to stay.

It would have to be Auntie Doll, Kenny decided, she was the best bet. He would set off for work as usual on Monday morning and walk up to Kirkholt and by that time — then he remembered that Doll worked and would be out of the house, which meant spending all day strolling about and killing time till she came home in the evening. He didn't even have enough money to go to the flicks: he looked on top of the cabinet at the side of his bed and counted seven and a half pence. The entire business suddenly struck him as being hopeless; he might as well own up and get it over and done with. He wasn't going to get any money, from Doll or anybody. An impossible scheme came into his head: he would break into Haigh's and rob the safe. He knew the layout of the place, where the main office was, and the exact location of the large old-fashioned safe with the brass handle. All he had to do was——

Kenny's brain stopped functioning at this point. It went as far as the works, the office, the safe, and then it stopped. His mind went as blank as the ceiling. There were times when he really didn't comprehend the world he lived in: when it became very confused and tangled-up, like a dream or a nightmare. What had seemed simple became complicated; he couldn't seem to get his thoughts into any logical or meaningful order and he felt that life was beating him down, that somehow he was being cheated.

His mother came into the room without knocking. It was Sunday night and she was all dolled up for the Kirkholt Social Club where Bernard Manning was drawing them in from miles around.

"We're off. We'll be late, so see Kat gets to bed." Her tinted hair was swept up at the back and she jangled with cheap jewellery.

"Is Brian going with you?" Kenny said. His body filled the narrow bed, stretched out amongst the chocolate wrappings. He crossed his legs and propped his wrinkled socks on the brown varnished tailboard.

"We're meeting Bill and Irene in the Dicken Green," his mother said. She made a face. "Kenny, your feet do smell. When did you change your socks?"

"Your nose is too near your arse," Kenny said.

His mother checked her reply. She hadn't time. "See Kat gets to bed."

"I might be going out."

"Well lock the door and don't be late back," she said, suddenly irritable. "You're bloody hopeless to get out of bed on a Monday morning." She sniffed the perfume on her wrist and went out.

"Margaret," Kenny said.

"I'm going to be late. What is it?"

"I've no money."

"Well?"

"Lend us a quid."

"I gave you some money the other night—Friday." Her voice had started to rise and Kenny prepared himself for a lecture.

"I can't keep on giving it to you. What do you do with it all? It wouldn't be so bad if you paid me back. What about that money from last week?"

"You'll gerrit, you'll gerrit."

"When?"

"Friday."

"I've heard that before."

"I'm skint."

"Well you'll have to stay skint."

"Miserable old cow," Kenny said under his breath, but loud enough for her to hear. Margaret came back into the room and lowered her voice. "If your father hears you talking like that you'll be for it. Here." She fumbled in her purse and threw a fifty-pence piece on the bed. Her face was pulled into an expression that was half-furious, half-conciliatory. She had never been pretty: her features were too coarse and ill-defined: her skin had a mottled look about it that came from poor food or too much make-up, or a combination of both. And it had always seemed natural to Kenny that he should bite his nails because his mother had bitten hers for as long as he could remember. He made no move to pick up the fifty-pence piece, but lay watching her almost with contempt, his slightly protruding eyes taking her in, summing her up, writing her off.

"Not enough," Kenny said.

"It'll bloody have to be enough," Margaret said, her voice thickening, "that's all you're getting." She pointed at him and several rings flashed weakly in the room's failing light: "And I want it back on Friday when you get paid. And what you owe me from Friday. And from last week. Think on."

Kenny mouthed 'fuck off' to her back as she went out and vee-signed the door several times with both hands. He sat up and without making a sound screamed every word of abuse he could think of, the words filled to bursting in his throat, their sounds in his head feeding his anger. At such moments he could have harmed her physically, he could have put the boot in, he could have stamped on her fat, dull, stupid face. She thought she knew everything, the old cow; if she only knew how thick she was. Kenny hated her for being so mean and petty: it was his own money he was asking for, his own money that he brought in every week, without fail, putting the pound notes on the kitchen table. And the miserable stingy old boot objected to lending him a measly quid. He picked up the fifty-pence piece and flung it as hard as he could across the room, where it struck the wardrobe door leaving a pale indentation in the walnut veneer.

. . .

When he comes out, still seething, Kat is in the living-room watching the television. She has fine fair hair tied up in bunches that stick out on either side of her head, like two clumps of straw. Her face hasn't been washed and she sits in the depths of an armchair scooping Rice Krispies from a bowl. Some of the milk has dribbled down the front of her dress.

"I'm going out."

"Awright." Scoop. Munch.

"Don't lock the door, else I can't get in."

"Awright." Scoop. Munch.

Kenny stops suddenly in the middle of the room. "Have you any money?" he asks.

Kat continues to munch the Rice Krispies but the motion of her jaws slows perceptibly. She shakes her head.

"You bloody have," Kenny says.

"I haven't."

"You fucking have. Where is it?"

"*Yav*-n't." Scoop. Munch.

He stands his ground watching the TV unseeingly, trying to remember where Kat keeps her money. Kids hide it in all sorts of daft places. There's a tea-chest full of toys in her room but he can't waste all night sorting through that lot. "Are you going to tell me?"

"Haven't got none. Honest." Kat fills her mouth with Rice Krispies. She won't look at him; her eyes remain fixed on the screen. She's a crafty little bastard.

"Lend it us and I'll give you back twice as much tomorrow," Kenny wheedles.

There's a momentary hesitation and he thinks she's going to give herself away. "Haven't got none. If I had I'd lend it you. Honest." She scoops up the Rice Krispies.

Kenny slams out of the flat having knocked the bowl onto the floor leaving her wailing.

. . .

Janice doesn't think it matters that he has no money; they can always go for a walk. "Walk?" Kenny says. "Where are we going to bloody walk to?"

"Walk. Just walk."

"Have you any money?"

"Thirteen pence," Janice says, offering it to him. She doesn't drink a lot, only halves of mild, so Kenny calculates that with his fifty pence he can afford three pints at least. Good job he's got enough fags to last him. They go in the Forester's near the junction of Bury Road and Mellor Street.

"Why didn't you come up today?" Janice says, settling back in the corner and looking up at him, her arm through his. She can feel his shoulder muscle working against her cheek as he puts the cigarette to his mouth.

"I'd no bloody money, had I?" Kenny says with infinite patience, as if communicating with a mental defective.

"You could have walked up."

Kenny pulls away to look down at her, sideways. "What's all this crap about walking?" he says. "Walking? I shouldn't have to bloody walk. What've you been reading, *Health and Strength*?"

"It's only ten minutes."

"Fifteen."

"Fifteen then."

"I shouldn't have to bloody walk. They don't walk. *She* doesn't walk anywhere"—the same bitter gall rising in his throat as he thinks back. He can see her dolled up in all her finery, sailing out to a club and leaving him with fifty-bleeding-pence. She wouldn't care if he had nothing: the mingy tightarse.

"Who?"

"The old lady," Kenny snarls. And then: "Forget it," swallowing half his pint before remembering that he has to take it easy. He bangs the glass down. He can't even have a drink without thinking about it. Money never really troubled him until he was without it. He had never visualised himself as having a lot of money, it was too far out of reach. He had never desired it even, as long as he had enough to get by. And now there was the job to plague him—or rather the lack of a job. Tomorrow he would have to start looking for one. Didn't matter what it was: anything would do to keep the old man off his back.

As if reading his thoughts Janice says: "Have you got a job yet?"

"Give us chance."

"What did your dad say?"

"He didn't say anything because he doesn't bloody know."

Janice snuggles against his arm. "You'll get a job easy. There's some advertised in the *Observer*. Engineers, fitters, loads of jobs. I bet you have a job by this time tomorrow."

"Yeh," Kenny says, far from certain. Then more brightly, "Yeh, there's loads of jobs." He picks up his glass and looks into it. In the end it all comes down to money. If he had money he wouldn't be bothered about a thing. He wouldn't have to creep about the flat like somebody scared of their own shadow. Even his own sister wouldn't help him out when he needed a few bob, and she always had money, given to her by Auntie Doll or by the woman next door for running errands; he'd even seen the insurance man slip her something just for standing there simpering, a jam butty stuck in her gob. He wouldn't half give it her tomorrow, he'd make her life a misery.

"Are we going to Wrexham next Saturday?" Janice asks, tipping her glass and drinking half a mouthful of mild.

"What with? Washers?"

"Me mum'll give me some."

"She won't give you enough for both of us, though, will she? I'm not going to have enough by next Saturday, am I? Supposing I get a job tomorrow I'm not going to get paid till next week, a week on Friday. They always work a week in hand."

"Won't Crabby lend it you?" Janice says. To her, Kenny and the gang are an indivisible, tightly-knit force standing against the world. In her mind she pictures them as a band of dare-devil marauders, all for one and one for all, and still finds it difficult to believe that they're willing to accept her — Janice Singleton — as a member of their mysterious sect and let her share their secrets.

Kenny laughs. "Oh aye, Crabby'll lend it me. He's rolling in it, Crabby." The sarcasm is laid on in great thick slabs, but even so Janice accepts the words at face-value. If he were to tell her that he couldn't make her pregnant because he was suffering from cancer it's probable that she would believe him.

She clutches his arm tightly and her upturned face catches the dim light from the red globes set in the ceiling. Kenny senses the quickening tempo, transmitted through her slim sharp fingers: she has beautifully white fragile hands which when resting in his are like pale leaves on a background of reddish sandstone. His hands are twice the size of hers, ungainly and heavy and blunt-fingered. His voice becomes low and thick:

"Is your mother in?"

"She was earlier on."

"Isn't she going out?"

"I don't know."

"Have you got a key?"

"Yeh."

"We're all right then."

"What if she's in?"

"What if she is?"

Janice smiles a slow, impish smile, at once coy and yet full of guile. She is a fledgling temptress fluttering scared little wings and daring to fly close to the flame. Kenny puts his mouth to her ear and whispers sweet obscenities.

"Is she under-age?" the landlord says, leaning over them with both hands gripping the edge of the table.

"What you on about?"

"How old are you?" the landlord asks Janice, ignoring Kenny.

"Come off it," Kenny says, "don't be so thick. She's been in here before——"

"I'm talking to her," the landlord says, not taking his eyes off Janice. "If you're under-age—out. I'm not being fined for you."

The blood is starting to rush in Kenny's neck. "I've told you, she's been in here before. Loads of times ——"

"That's a school blouse she's got on."

"Is it fuck a school blouse."

"It's a school blouse."

Kenny grips one of the landlord's wrists and says quickly and quietly: "Listen you poxy-faced gett. I've just told you. Are you

[74]

deaf? She was in here with me last week. You never said owt then."

The landlord straightens up. "All right," he says crisply. "Out."

Kenny pushes the table-leg with his foot so that the glasses rock about and slop beer. He half-stands, the hand with the knuckles labelled H.A.T.E. outstretched in a gesture that is both a warning and a threat.

"Kenny," Janice says in a whisper, "let's go."

"Any of that and you're for it," the landlord says, standing there and watching the large, raw-boned lad carefully but without fear. He's a fairly hefty bloke himself and he's dealt with bigger ones than Kenny. "Outside. Now. Let's have you."

"Kenny!" Janice says, tugging his sleeve.

Kenny picks up the glass and empties the beer on to the floor. He puts the glass down and with Janice trailing after him goes past the bar in the direction of the swing-doors. He doesn't use his hands but kicks his way through them. "You're barred from here from now on," he hears the landlord call in the hush.

"Go and stuff yourself."

"Sort 'em out, Ted," a voice says.

"Bloody vandals," the landlord's voice says faintly, the noise starting up again.

Kenny fumes his way up Bury Road. He can't stop his hands shaking. They reach the cemetery where Janice, not having dared to speak, succeeds in putting her hand in his, trotting along anxiously beside him. It frightens her that she doesn't know how to placate his anger: he is totally alone, face closed and eyes blank, in a mindless inner turmoil of rage and impotence. He doesn't even curse, which is the most frightening thing of all; she is expecting him to attack something, anything, an inanimate object like a lamp-post or a parked car or somebody's garden-gate. In the shadow of the garages down the rutted track Janice puts her arms round his waist and lays her head on his chest. Kenny leans against the garage, banging the heel of his boot like an impatient heartbeat on the creosoted timber, his arms hanging straight down at his sides and his fists clenching and unclenching as though to the rhythm of a pulse.

"Kenny," Janice says softly. "Kenny." She can't see his face in the darkness; the moon is hidden in cloud, occasionally glimpsed through wispy streamers, here and there patches of sky dense with stars. Traffic hums distantly on the main road.

"Kenny," Janice says, looking up, trying to tempt him into a kiss or at least an embrace.

"What?" There is no give in his voice, no slackness.

Janice breathes deeply and evenly. "Come on." She tightens her hold on his body, which is hard beneath her hands. At first he doesn't respond. Then his arms encircle her shoulders, the weight almost crushing her. The two of them remain like this for a while, passively holding one another, not speaking, each responding to the other's warmth and seeming as if to drift gently away from the world.

"Jan," Kenny says, coming to his senses, and overpowers her with a brutal kiss that shuts off the breath in her throat. His tongue is in her mouth, probing, insistent, tasting her saliva; and with her mouth inside his she finds herself struggling for air.

"Kenny——"

"Come on."

"Wait——"

"Come on!"

Before she can draw breath his lips and tongue are working on hers, hard and insensible, until she is smothering in his embrace. There is no escape. His hands begin their search for her breasts, encountering the stretch-nylon and the thin cotton cups and the small pink nipples whose response to his caress is guarded and unsure, eager and yet cautious and not fully awakened. His other hand goes between her legs, rummaging past her coat and under her skirt to locate the place where his hand can slip down her tights and across the firm young belly, warm beneath his fingers, towards the hidden cleft that it is imperative to reach. They stand awkwardly in this position, their mouths clamped together, both his hands engaged in foraging operations. Struggling for air Janice finally manages to break away.

"Kenny!"

"Uh?"

"*Ken*ny."

"What's up?"

"Not here."

"What?"

"No." She succeeds in removing one of his hands, the other still holding her breast.

"What's up with you?"

"Me coat's getting all dirty."

"So what?"

"It's for best."

"Oh, bloody hell," Kenny says with mock tragedy. "Her best coat's getting dirty. Oh I am a bad boy. Oh chop me hands off."

"It isn't that."

"It isn't what?" Kenny says, looking at her in the darkness.

Janice swallows. "That."

"That what?"

"*That*. You know."

Kenny doesn't know what she's talking about. "I don't know what you're on about."

"I don't mind you doing *that*," Janice says in a rush, "but not here."

"Oh." The penny drops. He doesn't say anything: it's up to Janice to make the next move. She buttons her coat and they walk along the rutted track towards the main road, leaning against each other. Near the flat where she lives Janice says: "There's a light on."

"Your mother's all right," Kenny says reassuringly.

Suddenly they hold one another very tightly, and Janice has the feeling she had that night they ran down Sandy Lane past the cemetery, her heart in her mouth, almost sick with excitement. Fluids gurgle in some mysterious part of her anatomy and she can't seem to quite catch her breath. Her hands are cold and in comparison Kenny's large rough paws feel to be on fire.

Mrs Singleton is alone in the flat watching a play on television.

"Where were you today?" she says as Kenny dumps himself in an armchair.

"Short of brass," Kenny says, sprawled out.

"You're always short," Mrs Singleton says, puffing on a cigarette. "I don't know. What with the amount you earn, you should be rolling in it. When I was your age we didn't have two ha'pennies to rub together."

Kenny cocks his head on one side. "Did they have ha'pennies when you were young, Vera?"

"No, beads," Vera Singleton says. "Cheeky bugger." She blows a gust of smoke into the air and stubs out the cigarette in a full ashtray. "Are you making this lad a drink, Janice?" she calls to her daughter; there's the sound of gushing water from the bathroom. Then to Kenny: "Are you hungry?"

"Depends what for," Kenny says stolidly, sunk in the chair,

Vera Singleton raises pencilled eyebrows above mauve eyeshadow. "You're all the same, you fellas. Your belly and the other thing, that's all you're bothered about." She lights a cigarette with an expensive-looking lighter; then as an afterthought throws a cigarette to Kenny. "How's your mam keeping?"

"All right."

"She still bingo-ing?"

"Aye, silly cow. Throws money away hand over fist."

Mrs Singleton sucks the smoke into her lungs with a sharp

intake of breath, already the end of the cigarette covered in lipstick. Her face is heavy, over-ripe, with the powder settling into the cracks and lines that radiate from her eyes and mouth and down either side of her nose: too many late nights and too much Guinness have robbed the skin of its bloom and tautness, and the dragging inertia of approaching middle-age is pulling wearily at her features so that it requires constant animation to keep the truth from showing. Her body is packed solid, like an overstuffed cushion: she seems constrained inside the clothes she wears as though at any moment something is going to burst and spill its contents over the rug. And yet you wouldn't describe her as fat; well-built, ample, a shade overblown perhaps. Janice comes into the room, a slip of nothing in her school blouse and grey pleated skirt. "Do you want a drink?" she asks Kenny quietly.

"Not bothered," Kenny says, looking straight at Janice, whose colour deepens as her eyes meet his. Kenny gnaws at his fingernails and his eyes flick back and forth from her face to the passage leading to her bedroom. Janice frowns and shakes her head slightly, and behind her mother's chair motions him to be patient. In the middle of this Mrs Singleton turns round.

Janice blushes and clears her throat. She says, "Do you want a drink, mum?"

"What's up with you?" Mrs Singleton says. She looks annoyed. "I can make my own drink, thank you." There is a brief silence. "Well?" she says. "You haven't brought the lad back at this time of night for a cup of cocoa."

MATCH

AT THE ROCHDALE V BLACKBURN ROVERS MATCH ON THE
8th December there was a crowd of 5,116, the largest gate of the
season so far. Kenny and Janice and the others had been in position
behind the goal since two-thirty — half an hour before the kick-off.
Kenny wore his blue-and-white striped scarf knotted onto his belt
so that it hung down nearly to the ground. At the other end of the
pitch the Blackburn Rovers supporters in their striped scarves and
bob-caps were massing: a sea of heads and upraised arms spilling
out of the low stand and down the concrete terrace. Already the
police had been in and removed three of them, to a chant of
"Ani-mals! Ani-mals! Ani-mals!" from the home crowd.

It was a clear blue brilliant day, a sharpness in the air, perfect for
football, the green turf stretching smooth and neatly trimmed in
the sunshine, and the breeze ruffling the corner flags. Queues
formed at the refreshment stands, waiting for Oxo and sweetish
coffee in plastic cups and hot meat pies wrapped in soft absorbent
squares of paper. Under the metal gantry in the main stand the
directors filed into the box, muffled to the chin in bulky suede jackets lined with sheepskin and double-breasted camel-hair coats.
With ten minutes to go the police had stationed themselves in front
of and amongst the crowd, nodding to one another while they kept
a careful watch on the pockets of potential aggression; the Rochdale
and Blackburn supporters were known to hate each other's guts,
having clashed at previous games both on the ground and in the
streets of the town.

"We hate Nottingham Forest.
We hate Liverpool too.
We hate Man. United——

But Rochdale we love you!" sang the crowd to the tune of 'Land of Hope and Glory', followed by the chant and counter-chant:

"Rochdale——"

"SHIT!"

"Rochdale——"

"SHIT!"

"Rochdale——"

Kenny and Janice were in the centre of a tight swaying mob about fifty in number, stabbing their arms upwards in time with the chants, an action that was dismissive of the away supporters and at the same time an overt threat. Fester, in-between surges, was drinking from a pint can of Long Life, the pale liquid gushing from the triangular slot — some of it, due to greed, missing his mouth and running down his chin and soaking into his crewneck sweater.

"Give us it, Fes," Crabby shouted.

"Get your own," Fester said, gulping beer.

"Tight bugger."

"Sod off."

A paltry cheer rang out as the home side ran into the sunshine, the smell of embrocation wafting on the breeze. They danced and jigged on the turf, testing their limbs like mechanical dolls released from a dark box under the stairs. Then a greater cheer as the opposing team trotted on to the field, rattles crackling like toy machine-guns, and moving bands of colour as the Blackburn supporters held their scarves aloft between outstretched arms, swaying to and fro, from left to right, their cries deafening the boos.

"Rov-ers! Rov-ers! Rov-ers!"

"Wait till half-time," Arthur said sourly.

"They brought at least ten coaches with 'em," Skush said.

"So what?" Crabby said with heavy bravado. "Rochdale lot could beat them any day. Eh Kenny?"

Kenny just grinned, the strong silent man of action, confident that he could out-punch, out-kick, out-stab, out-maim anything wearing a Blackburn Rovers scarf. Despite the cold (and it was only a few degrees above freezing) he wore a shirt with the sleeves rolled up tightly to the elbows and a vee-necked pullover: his neck and arms were pink and his lips were white, turning gradually to blue at the edges. With one arm he held Janice to him, their thigh-bones pressing hard. She was his girl; he felt strong with her beside him: the pride of possession and the smug knowledge of sexual conquest and the fist-clenching tenseness of the coming confrontation all mixed up inside him, generating a fever in the blood. It was good to be alive, the crowd surging forward to press against the barrier, the feeling of being packed tight amongst many bodies — and across the field of battle, the Enemy — a bond of antipathy joining the two camps that was almost a tangible force, something palpable in the air spanning the pitch.

A scuffle broke out down in front of them, directly behind the barrier, and the police moved in and hauled a youth head-first on to the red shale track, his shirt having been pulled out of his trousers and his braces dangling. He flailed with both arms but they pressed his head into the ground and dragged him away by the scruff of the neck. The crowd behind the goal seethed, like a large formless sea creature slithering about on the steps of the terrace, and the chant went up:

"Hooli-gans! Hooli-gans! Hooli-gans!"

Somebody threw a toilet-roll which uncurled in a fluttering yellow streamer and caught itself in the netting. At the other end the Blackburn supporters were cheering an attack.

"Have they scored?" Janice said, craning to see.

"I don't know,"Kenny said. "Come on."

He pulled her through the crowd.

"Where we off to?"

He didn't answer, holding her firmly by the hand and dodging through the spectators scattered thinly near the corner flag. A roar went up as they went behind the stand; they were on a narrow dirt-path, a brick wall to their right and on their left the grassy bank sloping down to the fence which encircled the ground. Kenny pressed his cold nose into her warm neck and Janice slipped her hands under his pullover. He could feel her trembling.

"What's up?" Kenny asked her. The gentleness in his voice came as a surprise.

"Cold."

"Get away." He curved his hand and held it to her breast. "You've got great tits."

Janice felt herself blushing, but at the same time his tenderness and solicitude pleased her; compliments from him were so rare and unexpected. Behind the wall at their backs the crowd moved restlessly, the roars and groans rising and falling in a continuous rhythm, seemingly for no reason. Kenny was feeling randy; he stood with his pelvis thrust forward so that the hard lump in his jeans would press into her. He moved his hips in a grinding motion.

"Can you feel that?"

"Yeh," Janice said, the word so soft as to be lost in her breath.

"Do you like it?"

"Yeh." Softer still.

Immediately she said this it became harder still and stuck out as far as his clothing would permit, and the blood-red mist glimmered behind his eyelids. He could have ripped her dress off, unzipped himself, and pushed it up then and there. Janice said:

"Oh Kenny don't."

"You like it, don't you?"

"Yeh."

"Well then."

"It's no use here. You know we can't do owt."

Kenny held her wrist. "Put your hand here." Obediently, like a good little girl, Janice pushed her hand between the two of them and felt him. "Fuckinell," Kenny said, shutting his eyes. Janice was breathing loosely and yet it was as if there was something binding her chest and preventing her from drawing in enough air.

Five lads were coming along the cindery dirt path towards them, walking in single file. Their heads were shorn and their trouser-bottoms ended just below the knee, leaving several inches of sock exposed; they wore scarves in their belts, which Kenny recognised as Bury colours; Bury were playing Swansea at home, so why they should be here he couldn't fathom — unless they'd been barred.

The one in front wore a bowler hat several sizes too small for him and had make-up on his eyes. Kenny thought: Another bunch of yobboes been to see *Clockwork Orange*. He pressed closer to Janice to allow them to pass, her hand still trapped down below. The lads went past, each lad staring into Janice's face as he did so. Kenny could feel their eyes on the back of his neck, like the burning sensation of the sun through a magnifying glass as the five stepped round him. The last one made a remark, which was enough.

The other four stopped, came back, and were all around. They had been short of an excuse, that was all, and none but the last had been bright enough to think of one.

"After tomming it were you Charlie?" one of them said.

"Rochdale lad," said Bowler Hat, plucking at Kenny's pullover.

"What a fucking team," said another, yanking Kenny's scarf.

"Does she do a bit then?"

"Had your end away?"

"Looks a dozy cunt to me," Bowler Hat said. He winked slyly at the others and kicked Kenny on the ankle.

"Shall we do him then, Mick?" one of them said.

Bowler Hat considered, and said slowly, "Yeah. Let's do him; then his bird. We'll do her too." He grinned at the others and leaned close to Kenny's shoulder. "What did you say?" he asked sharply, the smile vanishing. "What did you just call me? A dozy what? I'm asking you a question. What was it you called me? A dozy what?"

"I heard him," one of the others said.

"Are you laughing at me?" Bowler Hat said. He thumped Kenny's shoulder. "Don't fucking laugh at me."

"Let's have him, Mick."

"These Rochdale lot. Soft as shit."

"Nobody calls me that," Bowler Hat said. "Nobody." He wasn't quite as tall as Kenny, leaning forward on his toes, his eyes afire.

"You fucking try," Kenny said quietly.

"And?"

"Just you try."

"And?"

"Try it."

Bowler Hat hit Kenny with incredible savagery in the lower back with his coiled fist, aiming for the kidneys. Janice couldn't make out what happened next except that Kenny was rolling down the grass embankment with the five of them kicking him. At the bottom he tried to get up but was surrounded, all of them taking short steps backwards and running in to kick him. She saw Bowler Hat land one in his face and another of the lads edging round the back to kick him in the neck. They all had weapons of various kinds in their hands but weren't using them, concentrating on the boots. Bowler Hat was in a fury, shouting, "Nobody calls me that," and Janice was running — almost falling — down the embankment and hitting out at anything that happened to be in her way. She was screaming at the top of her voice and striking at heads and shoulders, not conscious of what she was doing, not feeling pain when they retaliated, aware only that he was on the ground and there was blood coming out of his mouth. She tried to get at Bowler Hat but there were bodies and limbs and feet in the way; something as solid and unyielding as bone socked her in the mouth and for a moment the world went away and she was in a kind of dream where it was quiet and misty, dark shapes seen through a haze. When her brain cleared the two of them were lying on the grass, Kenny on his back and she kneeling in front of him, dizzy with shock. He was dead, she knew it. They had killed him. She started to weep.

Kenny sat up and said through puffy lips, "Who do you think you are? Joe Bugner?"

Then he came out with a mouthful of foul language concerning the five Bury lads and the state of his face and the blood on his shirt; and Janice knew he was all right. At this she cried even harder until Kenny told her to pack it in.

. . .

"Jesus Ker-ist," said Fester, "what happened to you?"

"Me and Janice had a row."

"Bloody hell," Arthur said.

"Who was it, Blackburn supporters?" Andy said.

They stood near the refreshment hut eating meat pies and drinking coffee. The hot coffee made Kenny's gums ache. He hadn't lost any teeth but there was a nice lump on his jaw.

Janice said, "They were from Bury; they had Bury scarves on."

"I'll fucking bury them," Kenny said.

"I haven't seen any Bury supporters," Arthur said.

"One of them had a bowler hat on."

"Oh *him*," little Pete known as Shortarse said. "I've seen him."

Kenny was scanning the faces in the crowd, hardly able to contain the anger boiling inside, eager now to have a go at anything and anyone, it didn't matter who. He had the desire, but—like the Bury lads—he needed an excuse. Just a small excuse would do, a tiny one. His blood was singing and it was as though a million impulses were swirling about inside his head and spilling out of his ears ...

There was a commotion under the low stand: some of the Blackburn supporters were attempting to break through the thin cordon of police; high up on the banking above the terraces a policeman on a chestnut horse was patrolling the skyline; a sergeant walked along the red shale track with his eyes on the crowd, talking into his pocket transmitter. The P.A. system cleared its throat with a whine, a ping and a crackle, and Slade, fifteen times larger than life, crashed from the speakers fastened to the metal stanchions, and blasted the Saturday afternoon to Kingdom come.

Fester said: "They're breaking."

Kenny crumpled the plastic cup in his fist and leapt the barrier, amongst the front-runners as the mob surged like a black tide across the vibrant green of the pitch, charging towards the neat white goalposts at the opposite end behind which a pattern of pink dots wavered, shifted, and finally converged — like a family of corpuscles massing to repel an invader.

As he ran on the smooth grass Kenny took the steel washers out of his pocket and distributed them on either hand. He was sucking in great exhilarating breaths, his boots pounding along, others all round screaming and yelling, and he screamed and yelled too, the white framework of the goal square in his sights and the pink dots turning into faces with eyes, noses and mouths as he got nearer and they got bigger. But Kenny saw no face individually; it was a shoal of faces, a herd of faces, a pack of faces that he saw. They might have been Blackburn supporters, or Luton supporters, or Brighton supporters, or even Rochdale supporters: it didn't matter. Neither was he bothered as he threw himself in a full-length dive on to their heads whose body got in the way of his threshing arms and legs. He was like a machine having convulsions, four stiff limbs each with a steel-tipped extremity swirling like propeller blades, his bone head butting the faces, his body and thick neck jerking as if controlled by a mechanical brain.

Living things moved underneath and against him: soft, squashy, hairy, rough, warm, sharp, skin, cloth, leather, metal; yet Kenny was only aware of these things in the sense that they were outside of himself. He struck out at them passionately, almost with a kind of joy, feeling to be in the middle of a crawling, staggering mess of human life: at the centre of an experience in which all were equal, none were spared, each in turn victor and victim. When the flashing sharp razor sliced a clean red line on his forearm he recognised the pain but didn't feel it, straightening his left arm with the blood flowing down into the face in front of him, at the same time thrusting out right boot, left boot, right boot, left boot in a calculated ground-level attack. The steel-rimmed fists and the metal-reinforced boots might have achieved the necessary damage; Kenny didn't know and wasn't concerned; he was too busy elsewhere, head down, arms flailing, boots striking sparks on the concrete as they swung in a constant arc from front to rear.

From the way the ten hands took hold of him (simultaneously it seemed, like a ten-armed monster with lightning co-ordination) the thought occurred to Kenny that their object was to tear him limb from limb, ripping his arms out of their sockets and tearing his legs off as he had once torn the wings off flies before dousing them with petrol and setting their jitterbugging bodies alight. It was impossible to move, much less resist, with his arms and legs spreadeagled, his wrists and ankles held firm, and a knee like an iron wedge against his spinal column. He arched his body and bucked furiously, like a fish flopping about on a wet deck, and felt one of his arms go free; but as he was about to smile in triumph the monster took his testicles in one of its metal claws and squoze them. He nearly fainted. His neck went rigid and all the muscles seized up. He tried to scream but instead of words coming out bitter-tasting bile filled his throat and mouth, nearly choking him. As they carried him along the red shale track to the tunnel where the players were clattering from the darkness into the sunlight, Kenny — alone, blind and practically insensible in a little private world of pain and illness — Kenny could hear the sound he had lived with all his life: mingled with the roar and the cheering that greeted the teams were the jeers of the crowd: the sounds of hatred, fear, and derision.

HOME

WHILE IT LASTED THE JOB IN THE STOCKROOM AT Woolworth's on Yorkshire Street was all right; it didn't last long, however, three weeks to the day, because during the Saturday rush Mr Irwin, the store manager, caught Kenny sitting in the boiler room in front of the cold boiler he was supposed to be stoking, eating a half-pound slab of fruit cake and smoking cigarettes. As a job it had its perks: there were loads of birds floating around, and in the stockroom above the sales floor the racks of shelves reaching to the ceiling—'bins'—formed a labyrinth into which it was easy to slip away unnoticed for half-an-hour at a time. There was plenty to nick too: a box carelessly off-loaded from a trolley would split its corners and spill bars of chocolate or packets of crisps or slabs of fruit cake, several of which could be hidden in the tiny room above the lift shaft which housed the winding gear, to be consumed later that day in a moment of relaxation. Harold Marsh, the bloke in charge of the stockroom and Kenny's immediate boss (and not much older than Kenny), said Easter was always a good time because Easter eggs were that fragile and you only had to look at one of the brown cartons containing a gross to break half-a-dozen inside it; and smashed Easter eggs were no use to anybody, were they?

The part that Kenny didn't like was the humping—sacks of potatoes, crates of hardware, trays of potted plants, barrels of pottery, tea-chests of stationery, and endless brown paper packages which he seemed to spend all his days picking up, carrying, and putting down. Miss Crabtree, the woman who came up from the office to check the daily inventory, was a bit of a bastard too. She was a short, dumpy woman somewhere in her fifties who always wore the same two-piece grey suit and sensible low-heeled black shoes: she reminded him of the Israeli Prime Minister, and she would insist — though Kenny couldn't understand why — on his checking *every* item in *every* package to see that it tallied with the delivery note.

"What's the use of the note if I've got to check the stuff anyway?" Kenny asked her, and it took Miss Crabtree all her time to explain to him:

"That's what it's for, so you can check everything is in the package as it says." It annoyed her that he required an explanation at all; he was there to do a job, not to ask questions; anyone would think the system had sprung up without any thought, planning, or the most careful consideration.

It was the kind of job as well (which again niggled Kenny) that you never got to the end of: there were never any results, never anything to show for the work that had been put in. The area of scarred and pitted wooden floor from the lift-gates to the small corner office, with the rows of bins running off it, was never once completely clear during all the three weeks that he worked there. On Monday morning at about nine-thirty British Rail made its first delivery, and the area was filled with crates, boxes, cartons and packages piled ten deep, all of which had to be unpacked, sorted, checked, and the goods trundled off to be stacked on shelves in the dark maze of bins. Two hours later, say, having just begun to make a slight impression on the mountain of cardboard, wood and paper, the lift-bell would shrill and this time it was BRS with another jolly consignment that, for want of space, Harold and Kenny piled on top of the previous one. Thus the mountain grew.

By Thursday afternoon — Friday at the latest — the mountain had become an Everest, but by now they were making real inroads, undisturbed by fresh deliveries, and were able to reduce the mountain to a manageable hill, the vision of a bare space empty of packages now a definite possibility and not merely a foolish daydream. Then, on Saturday morning, their goal in sight, the potted plants and shrubs arrived: a full lorry-load that had to be shifted one crate at a time to avoid breakages. By lunchtime they had finished off-loading and — with the help of the girl in charge of the horticulture counter — had stacked the trays of plants against the wall of the cool damp cellar at the base of the lift-shaft, which left the afternoon to concentrate their attack on clearing the stockroom floor; but on Saturday afternoon it was one of Kenny's jobs to take the broom with the yard-wide head and sweep the sales floor, a job he detested because of the legs and prams and dogs that got in the way. This proved to him how stupid people could be. Even when they saw him with his broom, hugging the side of the counter, they wouldn't budge (the bastards), so he kept his eyes down and went through the lot, regardless of age, sex, colour or creed.

Harold battled on in the stockroom for an hour or so during the afternoon, tunnelling away at what remained of the mountain, but at about three o'clock he usually disappeared — either to eat slab cake in the machine-room above the lift, or to chat up the manageress in the staff canteen, or he sneaked out for a crafty stroll round the indoor market. Kenny never found out where he got to: the crates and cartons and packages and boxes remained unopened: the mountain — or what was left of it — was never ultimately conquered, and on Monday morning at half-past nine the lift-bell shrilled to warn them that British Rail was parked in the street, loaded to the gunnels with the first bad news of the week.

But perhaps the worst job of all, and the one that Kenny hated more than any other, was having to tend the boiler, and — the last straw — whenever it went out, rake the dead coke from the firebox and relight it. He came up from the boiler-room looking like a miner after a ten-hour shift, cokedust in his nostrils and stuck to his lips, his face grey and his eyes smarting. Mr Irwin got mad when the boiler went out because it meant that the store was without heat and hot water, but Kenny didn't give a toss for Mr Irwin: he never went near the boiler-room if he could possibly avoid it, and twice when he should have been shovelling coke went on the skive, sitting on the parapet at the edge of the flat roof, shivering in his brown smock and watching the heads of the shoppers in Yorkshire Street.

On the credit side there was Eileen. He had encountered her several times in the gloomy wooden passage which linked the stockroom with the canteen: a tall, thin, slightly gawpy girl who carried her body carelessly and who always had a blatant expression on her face. She was the kind that Kenny could stare at and she stared straight back. They never actually got to grips (Kenny being the puritan that he was) but once or twice came close enough in the dim cobwebbed light to confront each other with lecherous glances. Eileen worked on Haberdashery, and there was usually a conflict of emotions whenever Harold told Kenny to load up the skip and wheel it the length of the sales floor to Eileen's counter: on the one hand he was quite keen to have the chance of chatting her up, but on the other he went a deep shade of mottled scarlet because the items he had to deliver were STs — sanitary towels — or 'manhole covers' as Harold called them. Grinding down in the lift Kenny turned all the packets over so that the labels were hidden, then charged past Hardware, Horticulture, Confectionery and Tinned Fruit looking neither to right nor left, and wouldn't even meet Eileen's eye until the offensive packets had been thrown under the counter out of sight.

On the Saturday that was to be his last day there, everything that could go wrong did go wrong: when he arrived late at twenty past eight, instead of Harold waiting for him with a brew he found Mr Irwin pacing up and down the stockroom with a thunderous brow: Harold had rung in to say he was sick, which meant that

Kenny would have to take charge. Kenny knew that Mr Irwin was bursting to say something about his being late, but under the circumstances had decided to restrain the impulse. Ten minutes later the lift-bell drilled a hole in the morning calm when it announced the arrival of thirty-two hundredweight sacks of King Edwards, Lincolns and Jerseys. Kenny helped the driver unload, and was humping the very last sack along the alley at the side of the store when Miss Crabtree stuck her scowling face out of the door and said that Household Goods had been waiting half an hour for some lampshades to be checked off and would he get a move on. It was Kenny's turn to restrain an impulse.

He said, "I haven't had me break yet."

"No time for that now," Miss Crabtree said tartly. "The shop comes first, then you can have your break."

Kenny thought longingly of breaking her neck and went up to unpack the lampshades. The middle-aged woman who looked after Household Goods was waiting in the stockroom office with her arms folded and her foot tapping.

"I've got three customers down there," she said. Kenny turned his back. He slashed open the large brown carton with a Stanley knife, and lampshades — pink, blue, turquoise and gold (all with matching tasselled fringes) — rolled across the floor. "Be careful!" the woman said.

Kenny controlled his breathing. "Do you want these ... lampshades or don't you?" he asked. The lift-bell rang.

"Give me three of each," the woman said.

"I've got to check them off first," Kenny said.

The woman stamped her foot. "I've got customers waiting."

"I've got to check them off first," Kenny said, unmoved. The lift-bell rang: three long impatient bursts. Miss Crabtree came up the stairs followed by Mr Irwin.

"Mrs Thomas," Miss Crabtree said, "haven't those shades gone down yet?"

"He won't let me take them, Miss Crabtree," Mrs Thomas complained.

"Kenny," Mr Irwin said, "I don't suppose you've been to look at the boiler this morning?"

"We can't wait all day," Miss Crabtree said.

"I've got to check them off first," Kenny said. "You told me to check everything off first."

"That doesn't matter now," Miss Crabtree said. "There's customers waiting."

"I've asked him to let me have three of each," Mrs Thomas said, "but he won't."

"You told me to check everything off," Kenny said.

"You can do it after," Miss Crabtree said.

Kenny said, "But you *told* me——"

"It's out," Mr Irwin said. The lift-bell started ringing and this time wouldn't stop. Mr Irwin said: "Can't somebody answer that bell?"

"Can we have three of each?" Miss Crabtree said, "*please*."

"Don't answer it just yet," Mr Irwin said. "See to the boiler first."

"Isn't he going to do these shades?" Mrs Thomas said.

"Where do you think you're off to?" Mr Irwin said.

"For me break," Kenny said, walking to the stairs.

"Come on, be reasonable," Mr Irwin said. "First things first."

"I've already told him," said Miss Crabtree, "the shop comes first; then he can have his break."

Kenny went down the stairs. "If I were you," he said, "I'd answer that fucking bell."

. . .

Brian strides into the living-room, slight, spare, not an ounce of excess flesh on him, and lifts Kenny out of the chair by his shirt collar.

"You've been at it again," Brian says. "Own up."

Kenny blusters guiltily. "Own up to what? What have I done now? It's always me."

"Our Kat wouldn't have done it," Brian says, still holding Kenny, who's now on his feet, and bigger and broader than his dad.

"What? What have I done? Why pick on me?"

"*Brian*," Margaret says from the door. "We don't know for certain. Let him have his say." She looks at Kenny with a pained, appealing expression on her face: her son wouldn't wilfully lie or steal, she knows that.

"I bloody know it's him," Brian says, picking up his cigarettes off the mantelpiece. "I can tell with the look on his face. Where did he get the money from to go out last night? You haven't been giving him any, have you?"

"Have you?" Brian says when Margaret's reply is delayed. He holds the match an inch away from his cigarette and looks at her.

Margaret says quietly, "Only a bob or two." She comes into the room, softly biting her lower lip, wishing now that she hadn't mentioned it.

"Where is it? Have you spent it?" Brian stands with his back to the artificial glowing coals, balanced on his toes like a dancer or a featherweight: sharp as a whippet and twice as spunky,

"*What?*" Kenny says. "Spent *what?*" He gapes from one to the other, his eyes bulging in a dumb show of bewildered innocence. The performance is just that little bit too convincing; yet still Margaret has her doubts.

"You bloody know," Brian says. "The insurance money. You've spent it, haven't you? It was on the table in the hallway last night— one pound and ten pence—and now it's fucking gone. Katrina wouldn't touch it and I haven't touched it and your mother put it there, so that leaves you." He points the two fingers holding the cigarette at Kenny:

"You'll tell me, me-laddo, I'll have it out of you."

"Why is it always me?" Kenny says, feeling genuinely aggrieved. "Whenever there's owt missing it's always me gets the blame." His eyelids start to quiver and tears prick the corners of his eyes.

"Why?" Brian says. "Why? Because you're such a clog-head, that's why. A bloody pie-can. Who else could it be? Did you ever stop to think of that when you took it — who else it could be but you?" He blows out a sigh that is full of smoke and turns away in disgust.

"You should have come to me, love," Margaret says. "I could have spared you enough for a couple of pints."

"I never said it *was* me," Kenny says. He throws himself down in the chair, almost weeping,

"And you'll stop this cadging off your mother," Brian says, resuming the attack. "If it isn't beer-money it's fags. You lie around the house all day and then expect to go off boozing at night."

Kenny sulks in the chair. "Not my fault I can't get a job."

"Leave the lad alone," Margaret says,

"No," Brian says with a flash of coldness, "I won't." He's about to say that it's as much her fault as Kenny's — for being so soft with him — but he doesn't feel like embarking on a family feud. The thing that annoys him even more than the money being stolen is Kenny's stupidity: it's like an insult, a personal affront, to be reminded that whenever the Seddons stepped outside the law they did it as bumbling amateurs, almost wilfully inviting disaster to befall them. And he remembers too the night they picked him up, his hands cut to ribbons from trying to scramble through the broken window and dripping all over the floor of the Black Maria.

"I could have been mistaken," Margaret says, flopping down into a chair. She tucks her red mottled legs underneath her large rump and pulls her skirt down, stained from the cafe. Her streaky blonde hair hovers like an indefinite halo above her head.

"Don't bloody insult me, woman," Brian says, raising his voice. Anger suddenly runs in his blood and he strikes Kenny on the side of the head with the back of his hand.

The word "Liar" is spoken — shouted — but is sucked in by the carpet and soft furnishings, muffled by the lightweight internal partitions of compressed fibreboard. There is a flurry of movement as Kenny tries to make a break for it; Brian thumps him again, then restrains him, and Margaret gets between them. The next thing that happens is that Kenny's nose is bleeding and Brian and Margaret are engaged in an awkward dance in front of the uniform flames of the simulated fire-effect. The hearth rug wraps itself round their feet as they stumble a few steps together.

"Go and put a cold flannel on your nose," Margaret says over her shoulder.

Kenny hangs his head in the stainless steel sink and watches the red swirl away down the plug-hole. He moves his head from side to side, making a pattern of dissolving dots, and then experiments with a few drips over the dirty crockery in the plastic bowl.

"Oh give over Brian," he hears Margaret's voice say scathingly from the living-room. Kenny knows from her tone that she is confronting him with his own past, dredging up every domestic misdemeanour and marital infidelity and all the falls from grace since they were married. She'll next remind him that he has no claim on purity and innocence——

"Were you never a lad?"

Kenny nods. Or were you never a lad——

"Your mother's told me enough about *you*."

Kenny grins. Or that. It was always, or usually always, the same. Brian's voice over-rides his mother's continual, pounding barrage with a firmly stated: "He's a liar, that lad; he's bloody lied to me."

"All right then, he's lied, he's lied — have you never lied?"

Kenny smiles into the sink.

There follows a long and involved dialogue concerning the unemployment situation nationally, and why he's been fired from four jobs in twelve months, and what the hell has the Common Market got to do with it, and who's to buy the food week after week to feed a human dustbin, and already he's been in trouble with the police, and now it's the fucking Juvenile Liaison Officer (language!) he's got to go and see every third Friday in the month, and where does he get to every other week when his bed hasn't been slept in for nights at a time, and only turning up to cadge this and borrow that and *steal* the other.

"Brian-Bloody-Know-All!" Margaret says with a thin sneer of scorn in her voice.

Brian knows that he can't possibly win at this game: everything he says will be deflected, turned inside-out, upside-down, and redirected at his own head. Every word he utters is like a boomerang that sooner or later will come whizzing back at twice the speed it left his lips. He has two alternatives — either to explode into uncontrollable fury and yell her into submission or to pick up his jacket, slam the door, and shoot off to the Weavers.

Whatever happens, Kenny is safe; for the umpteenth time disaster has been averted. He will get a roasting from Margaret but he can handle her by the simple method of taking not a blind bit of notice of anything she says. And anyway, it's too late now: the insurance money (a measly quid and ten pence) has gone for good. They can't dock it from his wages because he doesn't have any wages. They're thick, the pair of them. Brian doesn't even know he's been staying at Janice's; Margaret knows, because she asked him and he told her, but she won't dare tell Brian — unless there's a big bust-up one Friday night, the two of them sozzled on bitter and brown ale, and in a raging temper Brian insists on knowing what goes on behind his back, and why everybody in his own family is so bloody secretive, and if that lad doesn't start shaping soon there'll be trouble.

When his mother comes into the kitchen Kenny is sitting at the table reading the *Daily Mirror* and eating biscuits out of the tin.

"One of these days you'll be the death of me," Margaret says.

"I should be so lucky," Kenny says, munching away.

SOCCER MOB RUNS WILD

ONE FAN'S FACE SLASHED
HOUSES AND SHOPS STONED

ONE FAN slashed across the face with a razor ... a couple injured by flying glass ... four windows broken ... toilets smashed ... a flag stolen ... and a director's box invaded.

This is the tally of trouble in and around the Rochdale Football Club ground at Spotland on Saturday during and after the game against Blackburn Rovers.

The summary of incidents collated by police read:

——Mohammed Khan, an 18-year-old Blackburn fan, slashed across the face with a cut-throat razor. Hospital treatment required, 26 stitches in the wound.

——Club flag lowered by some Rovers supporters. Flag recovered by police outside the ground.

——Home directors' box besieged by about 80 fans at halftime. Two climbed in among the directors.

——Fusillade of stones rained at the houses 2 and 4 Willbutts Lane. Windows broken. Mr and Mrs Brian Fielden, in the front room at No 2 injured by flying glass.

——Stones hurled through shop windows at 64 and 184 Spotland Road.

——Toilets wrecked at the Spotland Filling Station, Mellor Street.

——Gangs of youths charged through shops in Cheetham Street and Yorkshire Street.

At the end of the day the police had made nine arrests. Alleged offences ranged from wounding to using threatening behaviour.

And one police officer said: "We have had tough crowds to deal with in the past, but this lot from Blackburn is the worst in my experience."

It was as a mob of about 100 Rovers supporters charged down Willbutts Lane towards the town after the match, that the windows of two houses were broken.

Mr Brian Fielden, aged 40, secretary of the Rochdale Amateur League, had decided to stay at his home, No 2, because he "feared the worst".

Mr Fielden told the *Observer*: "I heard the next door window crash. There was a mob of about a hundred outside. Two stones came through our window and there was flying glass all over the front room. My wife was hit in the eye by a fragment. I had my hand cut. Believe me, it was frightening."

Mr Fielden and his wife, Pauline, aged 38, both went to hospital to have their injuries treated.

The spectators who got into the directors' box attempted to manhandle Mr Leonard Hilton, a Rochdale FC director.

A police sergeant averted what had all the makings of a riot by coolly restraining a ringleader and easing him out of the box with the minimum of force.

The Rochdale players also had to run a gauntlet of spittle, cinders and abuse when they returned to the field at the start of the second half. At the end of the match the referee was escorted off the pitch by the police.

Mr F S Ratcliffe, the Rochdale chairman, said of the behaviour he saw: "I think it was disgusting. Some fans even jumped into the directors' box but there was no violence. I think the idea was to get down into the tunnel that way to get to the referee. It was terrible the way people reacted."

GANG

THE GANG MET ON THE CORNER OF MILKSTONE ROAD AND
Tweedale Street a few yards away from where the old Victory
Cinema had once been (the building was now a warehouse); there
were eleven of them, including the girls, and they were out for
trouble. This part of town was Paki-land, the old grand houses
fallen to wrack and ruin and taken over by a whole colony of immi-
grant families. The windows of what had been corner shops selling
sliced bread and floor-polish were now heaped with odd-looking
packets bearing indecipherable labels and containing even stranger
foodstuffs: greyish-coloured beans, small hard red pellets, curly
white things like dried-up slugs, and what appeared to be old brittle grass-cuttings. Long sausage-shapes wrapped in cloth hung
from skewers, and in the dim interior cardboard boxes were
stacked several deep over most of the floor, squashed on top of one
another, with just enough room between them for a beaten path
from door to counter. At one end of Tweedale Street the pretty
architecture of a Mormon church marked the southern outpost of
the territory, while at the other it petered out in a maze of backstreets before the rounded dome of a Catholic church, St John
the Baptist, announced the ultimate boundary. Beyond the church
lay Drake Street with its pubs, snack bars, furniture stores, men's
outfitters and the offices of the *Rochdale Observer*.

It was the coldest time of the year — though the snow and hail
were yet to come — with a damp blue fog lurking in the alleys and
tumbling sluggishly along the gutters. Overhead the lights took on
a greenish tinge, and when you looked along the length of
Tweedale Street they vanished into an opaque glow, like a row
of torchbearers marching steadfastly towards an unknown and

mysterious destination. Buses with cloudy windows and sides running with condensation appeared and disappeared, wafting cold air along the pavements in their wake.

Kenny and the others stood in a shop doorway, smoking and scrutinising the faces of passers-by in the gloom. They talked amongst themselves of 'mugging' someone — as if the word itself, in classifying the crime so that it fitted an official category, opened up new possibilities. When you mugged someone you did it for a reason and not merely for kicks or out of blind chance. Fester was all for grabbing the first person who came along, thrusting him into a doorway and threatening violence unless he parted with his wallet. Andy said that that wasn't the way to do it: you had to plan things, like the police did, like crooks did, on TV. Get one of the girls to lure a Paki down an entry and then when you had him on his own in the dark, stick the boot in quick. He wouldn't have a chance with them all around him; they would scare the shit out of him.

"Yeh," Kenny said, lounging in the shop doorway, "that's right. They go mad for a white girl," and saw Andy look at him swiftly.

"Which one of you two?" Fester said to the girls.

Crabby said, "We could hide and watch them for a bit. See what the Paki does, whether he gets his dick out."

"So you can have a wank," Arthur said, snorting, which prompted Crabby to thump him, and they wrestled on the edge of the pavement in the glare of passing headlights. Kenny said:

"Stop farting around. We got to do it without anybody knowing it was us." He pulled Janice against him roughly. She snuggled under his arm.

"It's a bloody good idea, that," Shortarse said. "Get Cil or Jan to give them a flash——"

"Bog off," Cil said from the comer of her mouth.

"What's up with Virgin Mary?" said one of the lads.

"Who hasn't been inside your knickers?" asked Arthur rhetorically.

"Shut up, pig."

Arthur grabbed her and she tried to kick him in the privates; they spun round on the pavement, Arthur bent at the waist to protect himself, Cil hopping on one foot and kicking with the other. A man and a woman came along, stepping into the road to avoid them. The man muttered something and went on.

"What was that, squire?" Fester said.

Crabby said, "Are you talking to us or chewing a brick?"

Janice's arms were under Kenny's jacket, hugging him for warmth. She could feel the wide rib-cage, the tenseness of his stomach muscles, the vibrations of his heart. She wore a pair of black slacks and a new navy-blue blazer with yellow piping along the edges; Kenny could smell her mother's perfume. Her young bony face was somewhere below his shoulder, hidden in shadow. He felt strong, protective, invincible. She was his girl, all right, Kenny's bird. The fact brought comfort to them both. Janice said, "Are you coming back tonight?"

"Do you want me to?"

"If you want," Janice said quietly.

"But do you want me to?"

"It's up to you."

"Hey," said Kenny suddenly. "Come back to my place."

"What about your dad?"

"He's away working."

"What will your mum say?"

Kenny made a disparaging sound and flicked his cigarette away, as though any consideration of his mother's feelings was beneath contempt. The mist was thickening. He thought: Janice is just like the old lady, really. Dumb. Why were they all so dumb, women? They didn't know a thing. At least he respected the old man; but there again, *she* could twist him round her little finger when she wanted to. Kenny would never allow a bird to get the better of him. They were good for one thing but once you'd said that you'd said the lot. This put him in mind of Eileen, the girl on Haberdashery in Woolworth's, the one he'd never got to grips with. There was nothing to stop him having a stroll round there one afternoon: it was a public place, not much they could say, and if they did he would tell them to stuff it. She had that look about her, Eileen, that look of an older girl who'd been around and knew the score. There wouldn't be any stink finger with Eileen — straight in, knickers down, and hold that till it spits at you.

"Are we going or aren't we?" Arthur said, banging his forehead against the plate-glass window.

"Wait your sweat," Kenny said. He bit his nails and looked up the street towards the Catholic church which he couldn't see: the street-lights were now faint and blurred in the fog, like feeble glow-worms in a long blue underwater tunnel. The air was cold and clammy, chilling to the skin, seeping into their clothes. Occasionally shrouded figures came at them out of the gloom and hurried by, mostly couples.

"Fuck this for a lark," Fester complained, pushing into the door-way past Kenny and Janice to get out of the damp.

One of the lads said, "What are we hanging round here for?"

"Shut up, moron," Kenny said, immediately incensed.

They all went quiet as four Pakistani youths came along, walking to town, and in spite of the cold wearing thin cotton jackets and open-necked shirts. Crabby sniggered as they passed by, following them for a few paces and copying the way they delicately walked in their thin-soled pointed shoes. He came back, mincing along the pavement in his enormous red boots.

Andy gave Kenny a cigarette. "Let's wait till later on," he said. "The best time is after the pubs shut when they're coming back from town. They'll be pissed then and it'll be dead easy."

Kenny hadn't thought of this but he didn't want to give the impression that he hadn't thought of it. He nodded slowly, as if considering the suggestion and weighing it carefully; a random clutter of formless notions shuttled about inside his head, not one of them clearer or more distinct than any other.

"Trouble is," said Andy again, thinking aloud this time, "they might have spent up by then. They'll have nowt left."

Kenny nodded. He hadn't thought of this either. "Could be," he said. He didn't know what else to say.

Janice shivered against him, her eyes blank and staring out at the fog. With Kenny beside her she was prepared to wait till Doomsday, till Eternity, till The Cows Came Home. But Kenny knew he had to make a decision soon, he had to act. When you were the leader you had to take all the responsibility, and more than that, you had to be prepared to take risks. At the match he had proved to them—and himself—that while others hesitated Kenny Seddon got stuck in. And he was the only one who had to report to the Juvenile Liaison Officer: none of the others had to do that.

Suddenly be felt stifled. It came over him like a wave of weariness, as though the strength in his limbs had turned to water. It all seemed futile, as though there was no point in anything he did. He was in a closed, claustrophobic world of fog and thwarted ambition and stunted opportunity; he imagined it was similar to being trapped inside a strait-jacket, that sense of powerlessness and the inability to take action, either positive or negative, for or against. From the depths of the doorway Fester said:

"I feel like a bleeding brass monkey."

There was a chorus of complaint, Crabby whining and Arthur kicking the pavement.

Skush said, "Somebody's coming," and silence fell.

Kenny waved them out of sight round the corner and pushed Janice on to the pavement. She turned to look at him, puzzled and uncertain, rather lost on her own in the fog. Kenny stabbed his finger and withdrew into the shadow.

"Dirty sods, Pakis," Fester murmured in his ear, and it was indeed a lone Pakistani who emerged from the dampness and gloom, his head bent forward and his narrow pointed shoulders swathed in a woolly scarf. He hesitated when he saw Janice, paused in his stride, and was about to go on when she said something to him. Kenny couldn't hear the words but it enraged him that she had thought of something to say and that it was sufficient to make the man stop; it would have been better had she been too timid or had the man dismissed her and gone on his way. But he didn't, following her round the corner into the sidestreet and into an alley that was in total blackness.

They waited, Kenny and Fester, and then walked as quickly and as quietly as they could along the street and straight into the alley. It was slippery underfoot, the wet millstone setts sloping to a central drainage channel. They advanced a few paces, unafraid, trying to distinguish shapes; somewhere ahead of them were Janice and the Paki, and beyond them, presumably, the others. Kenny and Fester stopped, shoulder to shoulder, almost filling the alley, and there was an unnerving dead silence. Kenny couldn't hear breathing or the rustle of clothing or a foot scraping the setts or anything. It was as though an error had been made, that perhaps this wasn't the right alley after all. The Paki had worked magic and spirited her away, and Kenny was standing alone in the darkness listening to the internal sounds behind his eardrums and the deafening hush of silence.

And then a voice said distinctly, inches away it seemed, "Please. I'm sorry. Let me go."

Kenny put out his hand and touched a face.

Somebody started slobbering and moaning, but it was the kind of sound a child would make, not a grown man. Kenny felt for the lapels of a jacket and held them. He said:

"Give us your money. That's all we're after."

"Please," the man whispered. "Please…"

"Your money," Kenny repeated. "That's all we want. Give us your money. We don't want to hurt you. That's right," he said, feeling the texture of notes. "What's in your pockets?" The man fumbled, dropped coins on the floor, and Kenny took the rest and put them in his pocket.

"Please let me go. I am sorry. She asked me to come…"

The words tailed off into a wailing sound that was half crying and half a tuneless prayer, as if the man were looking to his heaven and begging forgiveness for his sins and seeking merciful deliverance.

"You didn't know she was my girl," Kenny said, "did you?"

The wailing went on, a quivering nasal sound that rose and fell with jarring monotony. Interspersed in it were words that Kenny didn't understand. He had hold of the man's lapels again.

"I bet if we hadn't been here you'd have fucked her," he said — the wailing went on — "wouldn't you?"

"No … no … please. I wouldn't."

"Wouldn't you?" Kenny insisted, not letting go.

"No——"

"Wouldn't you?" Kenny said, and butted the man in the face with the top of his head.

Janice moved away to stand with Cil against the far wall as the lads took turns going in methodically in relay so that everybody had a fair number of kicks apiece. The wailing had stopped. There were sounds — difficult to identify and not really human at all — which were like short, strangled gasps: like somebody with a fit of choking who can't properly get his breath.

At least this was positive action, Kenny felt, kicking the lump in the darkness. He had made the decision after all; they couldn't accuse him of not planning it right and carrying it out. He even forgave Janice — she hadn't actually done anything wrong, he reflected — stepping back to let Fester in. It had all been part of the plan. It had been necessary, her chatting the Paki up, in order to get him into the alley away from the main road. And the little skinny bastard — the bastard! — had actually had the intention of putting his thin brown hands inside her clothing and pulling out his obscene brown dick and very likely making her do something obscene with it. Kenny thought how true it was what they said about them: they really were lower than animals, and on top of that the smell of their cooking made him puke.

. . .

Later — when they had got as far away as they considered safe (and Kenny and Janice had had a cuddle as they walked along) — Fester led the way into the Ship at the end of Milnrow Road. He was beaming across his wide red face, glad to be out of the cold, happy to be near a bar with enough money for a night's bevvy freely available, and with the loose easy feeling he usually got after a spot of exercise. He looked down at the spattered toe-caps of his boots and rubbed them on the back of his trouser-legs.

The Ship catered for two separate types of clientele: the old never-say-die regulars who sat at scrubbed tables peering at their cards and dominoes through a fog that was thicker inside the tap-room than outside in the street; and in the other room with the big bow-window of coloured glass and the old-fashioned jukebox in the corner, a young crowd which consisted mainly of underage scrubbers off the Waithlands Estate (known as Tintown) and a group of boys who looked like left-overs from the Fifties: greasy quiffs, leather jackets, crutch-tight jeans and blackheads. Fester belonged with them somehow. His face and manner had a dated look, as though he'd stepped off a Bill Haley record sleeve. In comparison Kenny and the rest were fresh-faced kids with the bloom of youth still on them, and with an air of reckless naivity, like giddy young colts eager to poke their noses into life.

Kenny bought two rounds with the money and found that he still had three dabs left. He thought of keeping some by for the old lady—he hadn't given her anything for three consecutive Fridays now—but it remained a thought.

"We can have us a chippie supper!" Crabby said excitedly.

"It's only nine o'clock," Shortarse said. "Bags of time."

"Drinking time," Fester said darkly, keeping up the image of champion boozer.

Kenny was feeling good. His doubts had vanished, he had money in his pocket, the night lay ahead like an unplundered tomb. And he had Janice; he loved her and she loved him.

"Let's go to the Lake," he said suddenly. Everybody looked at him as if he'd gone crazy. But when he was in the mood to do something Kenny swept all before him. They drank up (Fester muttering something unintelligible), walked to town and caught the Number 8 bus to the terminus near the Fisherman's Inn. Strangely enough, it was clear up there, the stars like icy pinpricks and the Lake cold and black and silent beneath the frosty air. On the Rakewood Viaduct the motorway traffic buzzed like a quiet yet angry swarm of bees.

"It's the highest motorway bridge in England," Shortarse said.

"The longest," Arthur said.

"The fucking highest," Shortarse said, "twatface."

Andy said, "I didn't see the Greasers in the cafe."

"They'll be up," Kenny said.

"Where we going to drink up here?" Fester complained. "There's only the Fisherman's and the Beach. They won't let us in."

Kenny curled his lip at Fester. "Here," he said to Cil. There was a rosy glow in his stomach and there was nothing that could stop him. He put two pound notes in her hand and told her to go into the Fisherman's for a half-bottle of Scotch: she was older-looking than Janice and would pass for eighteen: he fancied her at odd moments—like now—but there was an unspoken understanding amongst them that she was Andy's. He wouldn't touch a mate's bird; not, that is, unless it was put before him on a plate.

Across the smooth dead surface of the Lake the lights of the Lakeside Restaurant shone hard and bright in the still air. A car's headlights flashed briefly over the water and turned a semi-circle to follow the dirt road which wound along the edge of the Lake for half a mile till it changed into tarmacadam. There was nothing moving in the Lake, not a yacht, not a buoy, not a fish.

"It's the coldest water in England, this," said Shortarse. Arthur scoffed. "It is!" Shortarse said, his voice an octave higher.

"You'll be telling us next there's a village underneath it," Kenny said, which was the resident local rumour, handed down over several generations.

"There bloody is!" Shortarse said, oblivious to the fact that he was having the piss taken out of him.

"And you hear the church bells ringing under the water..."

"You can!" Shortarse said. "I know somebody who's heard it."

"Get away," he was told scathingly by several of the others.

Fester said, "I didn't know that about the bell." Andy stuck his finger in Kenny's ribs and they laughed at each other.

A crescent of moon was coming into view, creeping up from behind the dark rounded shapes of the moors. Its steady, unwavering reflection lay in a clear straight line across the Lake. Out of nowhere it occurred to Kenny that the reflection wouldn't exist if there were nobody there to look at it. For a moment it gave him a strange feeling, as if he were standing a distance away from himself and could see his life as one amongst many others. Several things became clear—for just an instant—and then it was as if the water had shivered and the reflection had been broken and his thoughts fell down again in a muddled heap.

They saw the Greasers arrive on their gleaming machines: a roar of exhausts and their headlamps like big white eyes in single file.

"Six," Andy said, wiping the neck of the bottle and handing it to Kenny.

Janice felt the suffocation in her chest — of fear, exhilaration and the dreadful unknown. She couldn't understand why she, of all people, should have been chosen to be here in this place at this time. What had she done to deserve such good fortune? Actually to be here at the live happening centre where real events were taking place, and not moping alone in some lost, dead corner where life was a mere grey blur. Her friends at school were like sheltered little bunnies: they would be sitting at home now watching TV, or helping their mothers bake a cake, or if they were lucky, dancing to Gary Glitter at the Church Youth Club. Janice wanted to feel that at last her life had started, that the adventure had begun, and here she was in the middle of an experience.

Crabby said, "I bet them Hondas cost a packet."

"Who was it, did you notice?" Arthur asked Kenny.

"Do you think there'll be any more coming?" Shortarse said nervously.

The eleven of them walked along the edge of the road like the platoon of soldiers in a movie Kenny had seen called 'A Walk In The Sun'. He remembered that he had seen it one Sunday afternoon at Janice's, the two of them sprawled on the settee, Mrs Singleton sitting in the armchair and blowing out gusts of smoke across the screen.

When they reached the cafe they stood to one side in the darkness and looked in through the open door at the six Greasers innocently drinking coffee and talking with cigarettes in the corners of their mouths. Their lank hair hung down on to their shoulders and at least three of them had skin complaints. The proprietor was standing behind the makeshift counter pretending to be doing something so that he wouldn't have to leave the cafe unattended. The sound of a television jingle for garden peas could be heard coming from the room at the back.

All but two of the gang outside stationed themselves quietly in the shadow adjacent to the door, while these two — Kenny and Andy — stood in full view and each broke a headlamp by putting the heels of their boots through the glass. It tinkled daintily in the cold air as it fell to the ground. As three of the Greasers stood up slowly, a kind of bewildered astonishment on their faces, and then came out in a rush, Fester and the others stuck out their feet across the doorway to trip them up; anyway, that was the plan, but the plan didn't work, for none of the three fell down.

The one in front — a tall lad, over six feet — kicked Kenny on the knee-cap and Kenny staggered into the gutter, cursing and almost crying. The pain didn't seem to last long, because the next thing he knew he was scraping somebody with the broken end of a whisky bottle. There was blood on his forehead (somebody else's blood: he had felt it spatter) and it seemed that the road was filled with bodies. How could there be so many? Had more Greasers arrived on silent machines, coasting along the Lake road like black leather ghosts? Kenny tried to count the number of bodies but every time he got to four he was interrupted and his concentration was required elsewhere.

It must have been going on for at least a minute before he realised that somebody was screaming, like one of those sounds that by its intensity makes itself inaudible. Kenny saw a bright red gash across somebody's forehead and a curtain of blood blotting out the features until it reached the O of the open mouth, all the teeth ringed with blood and standing out very white like a row of beads. And then something clouted him really hard on the back of the head and made him mad. He went mindless, forgot the Greasers, forgot the screaming, forgot the blood, lashing out with boots and fists without seeing who or what he was hitting. He did remember, after a while, to use the bottle, but when he looked at the end of his arm it was gone. He looked on the ground for it but could see nothing except shards of broken glass, one of which had 'Lucas', embossed in it. His left hand was smarting, and when he brought it to his mouth it seemed that something was wrong with his knuckles—one of them, at any rate, which didn't appear to be in line with the others: it was raised up like the end of a knobbly walking stick. And shite, he realised, it was beginning to throb like buggery.

Several of the bodies were now lying down; Kenny ran at them in turn and put the boot in before running from the lighted strip of pavement outside the cafe and into the darkness in the direction of Smithy Bridge Road. He sucked his sore knuckle as he ran, scriking.

DRUGS

FOR SEVERAL MONTHS SKUSH HAD BEEN BREAKING INTO and stealing drugs from chemists' shops in and around Rochdale. He had a habit he couldn't break and there was nobody—no girl-friend—to haul him back from the brink. The situation was tragic and paradoxical: he took drugs because he didn't have a girlfriend, while the taking of drugs reinforced his isolation and increased his desperation; and had he *had* a girlfriend to help him overcome his dependence on blues, black bombers and sleepers, it is likely that she wouldn't have been required for that purpose, because he wouldn't have needed to take them. His head was in a mess and his life was in poor shape—like Kenny he had had umpteen jobs and couldn't hold any of them down for longer than a few months: the drug problem meant that he soon got fired, while his being out of work and therefore short of cash led to further black depressions which only drugs could alleviate; and having acquired the habit it reduced his chances of finding a job and earn-ing money—which meant that for several months he had been breaking into and stealing drugs from chemists' shops in and around Rochdale.

In the week before Christmas (which was mild, damp and depressing) Skush was admitted to Birch Hill Hospital suffering from an overdose of barbiturates. On the second day, after spend-ing two nights in Roch 3 Ward, he was taken to see Dr F——, the resident psychiatrist. Skush explained that it had been a mistake, an accident, that he hadn't meant to take an overdose, only get a good night's sleep. Why had he needed to get a good night's sleep? the psychiatrist had asked. Because he hadn't been sleeping, Skush had replied. Why hadn't he been sleeping? the psychiatrist asked.

Because he'd been worrying, Skush answered. What had he been worrying about? the psychiatrist asked. About not sleeping, Skush said. I see, the psychiatrist said, and in the same breath: Where did you get the tablets from? From me mam, Skush said instantly. (Part of this was true, anyway; his mother did take sleeping tablets from time to time, but when Skush had tried them they had had no effect at all.) After being kept under observation for one more day he was released, Dr—— asking him if he wouldn't mind keeping in touch, particularly if he felt the need coming on to take regular doses of drugs to make him sleep.

That night—the day of his release—Skush broke into a chemist's in Castleton and got away with several dozen each of Durophet, Ritalin and Drinamyl tablets in their small white plain cardboard boxes. They were impossible to trace, he knew; if the police didn't connect him with the break-in he was safe, and he made sure of that by taking every possible care and precaution: fear and an intense form of controlled panic had bred in him cunning and deceit. The plotting and planning to get what be needed and the actual physical activity involved had for the moment displaced the full extent of the depression which he carried round with him, and from which he couldn't escape. Skush felt it hovering there, like a large black heavy bird, waiting to settle on his shoulders and dig its claws into his neck.

What depressed him was this: that he couldn't understand how Kenny and the others knew instinctively the correct things to say to people (girls) while he had forgotten (never knew) the secret code by which human beings communicated with one another. For instance, he had studied Kenny's strategy for dealing with girls— simple, direct, crude—and had tried to copy it. But when he did the girls either ignored him or took his blunt directness as a personal affront and reacted as though he had insulted them. Skush couldn't fathom it out. Had he said the wrong thing or said the right thing wrongly? He wasn't deformed, was he? He wasn't a hunchback, he wasn't stupid, he wasn't an imbecile—so what was he? Was there something wrong with him? How come Kenny could get away with blatant and unsubtle advances while he was afraid to open his mouth in case he said the wrong thing (which he invariably did)?

Another instance: Fester and Shortarse, a couple of unattractive deadbeats if ever there were any, didn't seem to suffer the agonies of rejection that he did, yet from his own observations he knew that their failures and abortive attempts were equal to his. He had watched them clumsily chatting up birds in the pub and had squirmed at their shallowness and stupidity—and then been amazed when, occasionally, the girls responded. Or had they *not* responded, been equally amazed when Fester turned away with a crude remark and a beery grin, apparently unaffected by once again having been spurned and made to look a tool.

Skush was different. He couldn't bear it when the eyes of the girl he was talking to went cold and distant; it wasn't open antagonism he feared most, it was the cold glassy stare of indifference, as if she were looking straight through him, as if he didn't exist. So to avoid situations like this he stopped talking to girls altogether—apart from Jan and Cil, and even with them his conversation was monosyllabic and self-defensive. This closing in on himself evoked a nightmarish future for Skush in which his life had been sacrificed before he had had chance to live it. At certain moments it struck him (like a blow in the face) that the life he was living was the only life he had: if things were as bad as this now, what were they going to become? What about girlfriends, and engagement parties, and fiancées, and getting married, and buying a house, and choosing furniture, and having children? Were they not meant for him? Was this little shell of loneliness and anguish and quiet desperation the sum total of the future? Skush could think about this for just so long, and then thankfully he didn't have to think about it any longer. Three white tablets shrunk his head to a dwindling speck of light and his awareness of conscious reality would have had acres of room on the head of a pin.

"How much can we get?" Kenny asks.

"Dollar apiece," Skush says. He takes three large round pill boxes out of his pocket and counts the number of tablets; then calculates for a minute. "Thirty quid or more."

"Shit," Kenny says wonderingly, staring out of the diesel window. "Ten dabs each."

"You won't get that," Andy says. The three of them are on their way to Manchester, excited and nervous.

"Why not?" Skush says.

"You won't."

"Why not?"

"You bloody won't."

"I've paid a dollar each before now."

"You would," Andy says. "But you won't get that. You'll get half a dollar each or more likely three for a dollar."

"That's still a fiver each," Kenny says optimistically.

"If we don't get nabbed first."

"You're a cheerful bugger," Skush tells Andy. His eyes are like great watery brown marbles. "Anyway we're not selling them all. I'm only selling two boxes." He puts them back in his pocket. The train moves through the dark night, swaying and rattling between Middleton and Newton Heath. There's a girl in the carriage who keeps looking at Kenny, but girls who eye him up put him off; he's scared if they take the initiative.

"Where should we try first?" Skush says.

"Pendulum," Andy says. His dark skin is glowing and he looks very handsome. In comparison, Skush's complexion is paperwhite: his movements are jerky and frenetic like a doll slowly winding down, and there is in him the faint hard edge of hysteria. Kenny hasn't noticed anything he considers out of the ordinary but Andy feels be ought to say something, yet he doesn't know what.

This being Christmas-time, the Pendulum is packed to the doors, the low rectangular room crammed with bodies and the smoke writhing in thick layers above the assembled heads. As yet (this being before nine o'clock) nobody is dancing: a roughly square area of floor is set aside like a sacred patch of territory which can only be invaded when the time and circumstances are judged right. But the music pounds on — amongst the jostling bodies, through the thick blue smoke, against the dirty white-washed walls — as the three lads squirm their way to the bar and have the barmaid set up three pints of Tartan. Skush disappears into the crowd and comes back several minutes later jingling some coins in his pocket:

"Seventy-five pence," he says, "for eight."

"That's … how much is that each?" Kenny says.

"Nine pence," Andy says. "I told you, you won't get much more."

"Give us three," Kenny says, and swallows them with his pint.

"Your hand's still swollen," Andy says.

"You should have seen that knuckle the day after," Kenny says. "Christ it was out here. The bastard; he must have hit me with a bottle."

"Is it still sore?"

"A bit. Not sore: tender. I told the old lady I'd fallen down some steps."

"I bet it stopped you wanking," Andy says with a brilliant grin.

"I get Jan to do it for me."

"What does she say when you slap it in her hand: 'No thanks, I don't smoke Woodbines'?"

Skush smiles wanly and orders another round. Kenny says, "Give us a box," and goes into the crowd.

Almost precisely on the stroke of nine, a boy with short back and sides and dressed in an open-necked shirt, blue and yellow striped pullover, a pair of baggy trousers with turn-ups, and brown leather shoes with hard soles begins to dance alone in the sacred square in front of the battery of amplifiers, behind which the dejay sits in darkness with a turntable and a stack of 45s. The boy's dance is a composite of styles: be-bop and rock n' roll, African tribal celebration and Voodoo ritual — but at its simplest it is free expression: the reactions of his body to the raw soul music which comes blistering from the speakers and makes the air seem solid with noise. He dances alone, looking down at his feet, intent on the movements and rhythms, as though what comes next is as much a surprise to him as to the people watching. For a while he is the focus of attention, and then in twos and groups of three and four other people come into the square and begin to take up the dance. Very soon the floor is filled with jerking, swaying, weaving bodies. Everyone dances with concentration; it is as though this is the serious part of the evening, to be pursued determinedly and with single-minded dedication.

Kenny returns and stuffs two pound notes into Skush's top pocket. They grin glassily at one another and Kenny leans his elbows on the bar and looks at the small varnished wooden sign which says:

OLD GOLFERS NEVER DIE
THEY JUST LOSE THEIR BALLS

He tips the pint of Tartan into his mouth and feels the cold rush of liquid down his throat: the sensation makes his senses start to slide. The bar becomes a dull noisy blur and he feels a sudden, tremendously strong urge for Janice. If she were here now he could go through it like a hot knife through butter. She was the first girl he had properly had it away with — the first one he didn't feel awkward or embarrassed with — no clumsy fingers fumbling for the catch on a bra-strap, or struggling to unzip a pair of tight jeans, or trying to unfasten the buttons on the front of a dress which turn out to be solely for the purpose of decoration. In short, he didn't feel a fool when he was with Janice; they were like two children who together had made an exploration of hidden places — as though they alone had discovered certain secrets and were bound by the knowledge of their discovery.

They stayed at the Pendulum till just after half-past nine and then walked across town (it was freezing cold) to the Bier Keller on Charlotte Street, behind the Piccadilly Plaza Hotel. Down the green steps and into the dark smoky warmth where the Teds are gathered in sullen groups listening to Gene Vincent and Fats Domino and Elvis. They are dressed in drape jackets with velvet collars, close-fitting trousers wrapped tight to their ankles, and wear chunky wedge-like shoes. Their hair is glossy with Brylcreem, rising at the front in a smooth tidal wave and tapering to a DA licked into place and finished off with a neck shave. The three lads don't respond to this kind of music: to them it seems crude and obvious: Elvis's whining falsetto trying to reach the high notes on *That's All Right Mama* and Gene Vincent hiccuping to *Blue Jean Bop*. But there's a ready market and a good sale to be had here for blues and black bombers; the Teds won't touch acid or grass but rely on lager and pills to give them a charge.

Skush has lost interest in the proceedings and sits in a corner with a totally blank expression. The music reverberates inside his head, several light-years removed from that part of his brain which registers conscious reality. Kenny approaches a tall scowling youth with a boil on the end of his nose and thick sideburns that almost meet under his chin. He negotiates a deal and collects one pound and forty pence in fifty and ten pence pieces.

"How you doing?" Andy says when they meet back at the table.

"They're a load of twats," Kenny says succinctly.

"Won't they buy?"

"They'll buy anything; we should have mixed aspirin in with them, they'd never know the difference. What's up with him?" he says, nodding at Skush.

"Blocked to the eyeballs. Leave him be."

"We'll have to carry him to the station."

"We can get a taxi."

"Aye," Kenny says, his face slowly lighting up, "we can."

By the time eleven-fifteen comes round the three of them are staggering through the frosty grass in Piccadilly Gardens, tripping each other up and giggling like schoolgirls: they have the mistaken notion that they're walking to Victoria Station when in fact they're going in the direction of Albert Square. On Mosley Street a passer-by stares just a fraction too closely at their antics and Kenny follows him and grabs the back of his collar and thrusts him bodily against the wall. He's never felt more in the mood to batter a face in than right now.

He says sneeringly into the face of the man, "Did you get a good look or do you want a photograph?" And then says, "Cunt," and goes on repeating, "Cunt. Cunt."

Fucking Jesus, he wants to hit the man. Fucking Cunting Christ, the man's pale frightened face sickens him so much that nothing would feel better than kneeing him in the bollocks and seeing that awful fear he loves and yet despises turn into pain. He can see it in his mind's eye — the face crumbling as the pain reaches up from the groin and shoots into the brain.

An arm is holding Kenny and he knocks it away. The arm comes across his chest and he knocks it away again. He keeps repeating the one word, 'Cunt', over and over, his face inches away from the man's.

"Come on," says a slurred voice in his ear. Kenny's large hands are bunching the man's collar under his chin: the man hasn't said a word: he is trying to keep his face under control.

"Ken," the slurred voice says in his ear.

"Cunt," Kenny says. He wants the man to struggle, to resist, but the man is like a rag doll. The instinct of self-preservation tells him that Kenny is short only of an excuse; by adopting the line of least resistance he hopes to make himself unworthy of Kenny's attention, not even worth the effort of duffing up.

"Listen, cunt——"

"Kenny, come *on*," Andy says, dragging him along the empty street.

"Cunt."

"Yeh."

"Cunt."

"Yeh. Come on."

The city is like a grey dream. Buildings disappearing into the darkness overhead, intersected by rivers of gleaming tarmac. They walk along Princess Street, past the side of the silent Town Hall, into Albert Square. Everything is asleep, lost, dead, forgotten. The beacons at the crossings flicker on and off. Skush stumbles into the gutter and falls against the edge of the kerb. He might as well just lay here and die; it is a fitting end. People will be sorry when they hear of his death, they will wish they had treated him better, taken notice of him. It is all their fault. He knows that he hasn't yet begun to live and already he is dying. He wishes there was a girl here who could watch him die. The others pick him up and carry him along but he knows he is still in the gutter. They can't fool him, although they might think they're pretty smart.

There's a window in front of him which he knows isn't really a window at all: it's the bottom of a deep hole down which he is falling. He sees Kenny's lips move and the sound takes a long time to travel the distance to his ear and when it arrives it is slowed down in time with his heartbeats.

"Old golfers never die..." the words say.

Golfers. The word is irresistibly funny to Skush. He can see mechanical men swinging clockwork sticks — hundreds of them in unison. They are walking stiffly in ranks along the gutter, dropping in row after row down the deep, dark hole. He starts to giggle and the others giggle with him. All three are giggling as they fall towards the glass-bottomed hole.

"... they just lose their balls."

Skush holds out his fists straight in front of him and is the first to break through the glass-bottomed hole. It is a new world: bright, glistening, sharp, and filled with ladies' hats. He knows with part of his mind that Kenny and Andy are moving fast but to him they appear to be moving with the wearying slowness of a dream. Is this death? Is he dead? If he is they must have bells in heaven because — quite distinctly — he can hear them ringing.

"Fucking come on!" (Kenny speaking.)

"Get out of it." (Andy.)

"Get him."

"They're here."

"Leave him."

Three Panda cars are standing at strange angles at the kerb and five policemen pick Skush out of the wreckage, setting him on his feet in the middle of the pavement. One of them looks quickly round the deserted square and slams a fist into his kidneys. Skush goes down into the gutter and slowly gets up again, without assistance. Another of the policemen moves casually to one side and kicks him on the point of the ankle-bone; Skush yelps and goes down on his knees: they set him up again.

"Where's your mates?"

"Golfers," Skush says.

A policeman stands directly in front of him and shines a light in his eyes. "Why don't you fight back, laddie?" He turns to the others and says, "Get the van," and turning back to Skush clubs him across the ear with the torch.

"Balls," Skush says, shaking his head a little to clear the buzzing noise.

"Well laddie," the policeman says, "why don't you fight back? Eh? Come on, hit me."

"I'm only small," Skush says (which is true).

"Come on, laddie," the policeman says, and smashes the torch against the other ear. Skush nearly goes down but they save him from falling.

"Not on the head," one of the other policemen says. They are all young, strong and clean-shaven, and giants compared to Skush. The policeman is about to have another go when the van arrives. It has mesh across the windows. They carry Skush to the back of the van and throw him in. A fat policeman in a flat hat with a shiny peak shuts the doors and sits down on the bench-seat. Skush raises his head from the floor and looks at the policeman's shoes. He notices they have crepe soles.

"Are you all right?" the fat policeman asks, supporting him under the arms and lifting him to an upright position; and then before Skush can reply knocks him down again.

VERA

ON NEW YEAR'S EVE—A MONDAY—KENNY HAD HIS TEA AT Janice's and then with Janice and her mother went on the booze. It was very cold, the real chill of winter holding the town in an icy grip. They caught a bus to the town-centre and got off outside the General Post Office as the Town Hall clock was striking half past eight. Vera was full of revelry, perfumed, talcumed and all dolled up, expansive with the promise of the evening's festivities to come. Janice was wearing make-up and under her coat had on a multi-coloured blouse in silken material and a full-length black skirt; Kenny was wearing a suit. He linked arms with the woman and the girl and they turned the corner to Yates's Wine Lodge. It seemed to Kenny that half the men in the room looked up and nodded to Vera as they came through the swing-doors: she was popular, all right, which might explain (he thought) why she was never short of money despite not having a job.

"Hello Vera," a man said. "Can I buy you a drink?"

"I'm with me daughter tonight, Harry, and her boyfriend."

"Well?" Harry said. "It's New Year. What are you having?"

This was going to be a good night, Kenny decided.

"I'll have a tot," Vera said.

"Oh aye," Harry said. "Living in hope, eh?" Nudge-nudge, wink-wink.

"Brandy," Vera said, giving him the smile he expected. "What do you two want?"

Kenny had a pint and Janice a sweet sherry and the man brought the round to the table. A couple of old slags were sitting nearby, crouched over their schooners of Australian White Wine, like two crows concealing something unpleasant under their black folded wings. Kenny had only been in Yates's once or twice before: it was the refuge of the aged and decrepit and of those who would rather spend money on a night's drink instead of food for the next day; and of course it was the prime picking-up shop for those who weren't young any more.

"What do you do?" Harry said to Kenny.

"How do you mean?"

"For a job."

"Fuck all," Kenny said.

"Don't you work?"

"Not if I can help it."

The man wasn't too pleased with this answer. Lancashire folk don't take kindly to loafers, parasites and shirkers. Vera threw back the brandy with a practised hand and banged the glass down.

"My round," she said.

Kenny didn't argue, but went to get them, standing in line behind the chest-high wooden barrier which formed the drinkers into a queue so that each customer would be dealt with strictly by rota; it was a bit like queueing for the dole. Yates's ran a tight ship: drinking was a serious business.

He walked back with the tray across the bare boards, stepping round the groups of people who stood sipping their drinks. The place had an air of tired and somewhat desperate conviviality, as though all the people here were seeking shelter from the cold modern world outside by returning to the nineteenth century. They wouldn't have been out of place in a sepia photograph.

"A quiet lass," Harry observed of Janice.

"Takes after me," Vera Singleton said, flashing him a brief vivid smile, her bracelets glinting and jangling as she rummaged in her handbag for cigarettes and lighter. Somebody came up and whispered in her ear and she gave a bellow of laughter.

There was a world of experience in her laugh that was completely alien to Kenny, although he had heard that laugh a hundred times from as many women in dozens of public houses. It reminded him—for a reason he couldn't place immediately—of a cold and lonely time waiting for someone. It reminded him of sitting on a doorstep in short trousers, the dank misty gloom of a November night pressing against his face and bare legs, waiting on the step of number twenty-two Cayley Street, the door locked, for his mother to come click-clacking along the pavement in her stiletto heels, returning from a mysterious night out in the equally mysterious night-time town of Rochdale.

He remembered it clearly now: the old man had gone away, on business so his mother had said, and that one simple fact seemed to have altered the entire pattern of his life. For one thing there never seemed to be any food in the house. He went to the cupboard and looked behind the cups and saucers and plates for anything that was edible. He stood on a chair and looked in the bread-bin and then in the meat-safe at the top of the cellar steps, but all he could ever find were greasy margarine wrappers and bits of what looked like an old pork pie. Another memory stirred: of sitting up in bed, alone in the house, reading the *Dandy Annual* or *Boys Amazing Stories*, his eyelids tight and stinging for want of sleep but sticking it out till he heard the key in the lock and the front door scraping over those three lumps in the red and green linoleum.

And before she returned, the silence of the house—silent except for the creaking—silence extending beyond the bedroom door to the steep, dark stairs leading down to the kitchen which was forbidden and frightening territory. He would tiptoe to the bedroom window and look through the leaded panes at the street light shining on the stone setts, rubbing each foot alternately on the other to lessen the chill contact of the lino.

"I bet Kenneth's a randy beast," Vera Singleton said, a little the worse for the five brandies she had consumed.

Janice reddened and hid behind her glass of sherry; Kenny awoke from his stupor. "I know what it's all about," he said in a slurred voice.

"We're not letting the New Year in here," Vera said.

"They'll be shutting before twelve," Harry said.

"That's what I said. Come on. Drink up."

"Where to?" Harry said in-between swallows.

"Marlborough Con Club."

"Where's that?"

"Oldham," Vera said. "You've got a car, haven't you? Well then."

It was gone eleven when they arrived at the Marlborough Conservative Club on Abbey Hills Road and at first the man on the door wouldn't let them in. Then he recognised Vera and the four of them sailed into the smoke and noise of a couple of hundred people, many of whom seemed to have brought their children with them. Because of the crush the billiard table had been draped with a brown dust sheet and families sat around it eating sandwiches and cakes off paper plates. Vera disappeared for ten minutes, and when Janice went to the toilet she came across her mother talking to a man outside the ladies' lavatory.

"Won't be a minute, love," Vera said. "Tell Harry to get some drinks in."

"Who's this?" asked the man. He was fleshy and middle-aged and wore a ring with a stone that sparkled under the bland fluorescent lighting.

"Our Janice," Vera said, smiling and cuddling Janice's shoulder under her arm.

"Well well."

"Eyes off, you," Vera said. "Randy bugger." She gently propelled Janice forward a few paces. "I won't be a sec, love," she mouthed. "Get me a brandy, all right?"

"What a dump," was the first thing Kenny said when she got back to the table.

"What's up with it?" Janice said, edging up to him and leaning her elbow on the table so that their shoulders touched.

"Look at them," Kenny said; he was flushed and slightly drunk. "Guzzling. That's all they can do. Guzzle."

"So are you."

"That's all they're good for," Kenny said, ignoring her. "Useless, the lot of them. Neither use nor fucking ornament." His foot kicked out in a sudden fit of temper and a chair fell over. Several heads turned.

"Kenny, not here."

"What?" He narrowed his eyes and peered at her hazily as though through a cloud of smoke. There was a dribble of saliva on his chin.

"It's New Year's Eve."

"So fucking what?"

"Same again?" Harry said, standing up, his tie hanging on his belly and his belly hanging over the table.

"Aye," Kenny said. "Pint."

"Me mum wants another brandy," Janice said.

"Where's she got to?" Harry wanted to know.

"In the ladies'," Janice said with hardly a flicker of hesitation.

Midnight approached, the funny hats were put on, the coloured paper streamers stockpiled on each table ready for the fray. Kenny refused to join hands when *Auld Lang Syne* was played and sat staring sullenly at the rows of people swaying to and fro, their beer-glazed faces opening and shutting in what to him was a mindless, pointless exercise. The waste of it all appalled him: what did it mean, what was its purpose — this guzzling, shouting, screaming, endlessly *consuming* mob hysteria? They were like a pack of animals, with no other desires than to feed their appetites and indulge their bodily sensations. He was sickened. Janice watched him fearfully. It seemed that his only reaction nowadays was instant, savage emotion leading, sooner or later, to violence. She wondered why he couldn't settle down a bit; she wanted him to. She slipped her hand into his but his own hand remained passive, disinterested; she stroked his palm with her fingertips but there was no response.

Vera and Harry were in the line, singing away. Then, the New Year safely in, the line transformed itself and changed direction, from linked hands to clasping the waist of the person in front, from *Auld Lang Syne* to the Conga.

Kenny watched them with a sneer on his face. This pathetic charging about was what amused people. This was what he had to look forward to when he got old and past it. It was obvious to him what they were: they were all dead thick.

. . .

Harry stopped the car outside the flat, and before he could get out Vera said, "Thanks Harry. All the best now. Goodnight." He sat puzzled behind the wheel for a moment and then drove off. "Silly sod," Vera said, pulling a bunch of keys out of her handbag.

"Why do you bother with him?" Janice asked.

"He's a good payer, that's why," Vera said. She came between her daughter and Kenny and put her arms through theirs. "Come on, future son-in-law," she said. "Up the wooden hill."

"Have you any booze in?" Kenny said. He stumbled over the doorstep and went sprawling into the small dark hallway at the foot of the stairs.

"You're pissed," Vera told him.

"I was fucking tripped," Kenny mumbled.

"Language," Vera said. With Janice's help she hoisted him to his feet and somehow or other they got him to the top of the stairs. He was a dead, floundering weight, crashing into the door jamb and rebounding into the living-room, carried forward by his own momentum. They manoeuvred him into an armchair and dumped him, his head lolling about and his arms hanging down on either side.

"It's freezing in here, mam," Janice said.

"I should have left a bar on. Do you want owt to eat? Kenny, are you hungry?"

"Aye," Kenny said, hardly able to form the word. His lips felt numb, as though they were made of rubber. He put his hand up and touched his face and it was like a stranger's hand touching a mask. "I'll have a chicken butty."

"It's turkey," Vera said. "Janice, go and put the blanket on in my bed." She picked up her handbag to get cigarettes and all the contents fell out. "Shit," she said softly, and got down unsteadily on to her knees to shovel them back in.

Kenny started snoring, his head on one side, his mouth hanging open. It was a shallow, dreamless sleep and he came instantly awake when Janice gently nudged his foot. She was standing in front of him with two rounds of sandwiches on a plate and a beaker of coffee.

"Would you like a leg?" Vera called from the kitchen.

"I would that," Kenny said.

"I mean a leg of turkey. Randy bugger."

"This'll do me."

Vera came into the living-room and sat on the carpet in front of the electric fire. "I haven't been warm all night. Did you put that blanket on?" she said to Janice.

"You know a lot of folk in Rochdale," Kenny said.

"I know a lot of folk all over. I've known Harry for donkey's years. Divorced. Used to be a smart fella at one time but he's gone to pot. Boozes too much. Janice, get me fags, love." She tossed one to Kenny and lit one herself. "I suppose you're still traipsing down to the police station every month."

"Waste of bloody time," Kenny said. "I have to see this bird, Miss T——. I don't know what for. She parrots on for half an hour and then I piss off home. Useless."

"You said she keeps asking if you're working," Janice said.

"They've nowt better to do, some of them," Vera said. "All this crime about, cars being pinched, and they have to pick on ordinary folk. We nearly had a break-in here, did Janice tell you?"

"Yeh."

"Nobody saw him but the lock on number two had been damaged. Somebody trying to get in obviously."

"Did you report it?"

"And have them clod-hopping through the place? Did I buggery. Less I see of them the better. Anyway there's nowt worth pinching in the other flats at the moment, they're empty. There's a tenant moving in next week."

Kenny looked at Janice and winked. "I'm tired," he said. Janice bent down quickly to hide her face and started picking up plates. Vera said, "I bet it's freezing out."

"We'll all have to sleep in your bed," Kenny said.

"You might as well; that small bedroom will be like Siberia." Kenny, didn't know whether or not to take her seriously. She noticed his expression and said, "You're part of the family, aren't you? Well, almost."

"*Mum*," Janice said, frowning.

"Oh don't be so mard. You young ones today, I don't know. When I was a kid there were five of us in one bed."

"Brothers and sisters."

"Not always," Vera said, getting up and putting a cup and saucer on the coffee table. "Me uncle Arthur used to sleep with us sometimes. Christ, did he snore. *And* he used to take up half the bed."

Kenny waited in the living-room while Janice and her mother

got into bed, then went into the bedroom, stripped down to his underpants and climbed in beside them. It was lovely and warm and he was so tired he nearly went straight to sleep, but the presence of Janice, soft and vulnerable and pressed so close against his body immediately aroused him. He put his hand under her nightdress and she went rigid and stopped breathing. She put her mouth to his ear and said, "Wait," in the lightest of breaths. They lay with their eyes shut and their arms intertwined, listening to the alarm clock's relentless hollow tick and the mother's breathing getting slower and slower. Kenny was struggling with a massive erection and could feel the sweat gathering on his neck: he took Janice's hand and moulded her fingers around the aching stiffness: she held on to him as they waited in an agony of impatience.

"She must be asleep by now," Kenny whispered.

"Wait."

"Fuckinell, Jan."

"Sssshhh!"

It was torture; it was worse than torture. The lower part of his abdomen felt as if it contained a lump of concrete with an iron rod embedded in it. They began to kiss and touch each other and soon it didn't matter whether Janice's mother was awake or not. Kenny eased himself astride her and slowly the rhythm built up — both of them making sounds that neither were fully aware of. Kenny was dog-weary and kept falling into a dreamlike doze, the movement and the feeling going on separately, as it were, while he himself slept.

"Oh Kenny …" Janice said as she felt him coming inside her. "I love you … I love you."

The realisation of the actual physical moment, of the girl beneath him, brought him to his senses and he went on and on, harder, his stomach quivering and the insides of his legs jerking as he finally expended himself.

"Do you love me?" Janice asked softly.

"Yeh," Kenny said, extricating himself. He lay on his back in the hollow of the bed, the beer and the warmth and the tiredness pressing down on his limbs. He could have slept forever.

"Kenny," Janice said. "Say you love me."

"Mm," Kenny mumbled.

"Go on, Kenny, say it. Please."

"I love ..." Kenny said, and was asleep.

It was as though he hadn't slept ten minutes (he was sure it hadn't been an instant longer) when he felt something moving on his stomach. It felt like somebody's fingers.

"Are you awake?" a voice said. He didn't answer, but his body had tensed.

"Randy beast," Vera murmured, her hand slipping between his legs and cradling his balls.

ATTACK ON PAKISTANIS WHO
WANTED TO HELP GIRLS

JUDGE SENTENCES EIGHT
'BRUTAL COWARDS'

THINKING that a group of girls were being subjected to unwelcome attention from some youths, three Pakistani men stopped their car to speak to the girls.

They were then stoned by the youths and one had his skull fractured, Manchester Crown Court heard on Wednesday.

Sentencing eight youths for offences of affray and wounding Judge Desmond Bailey said: "You behaved in a wanton, cowardly and brutal fashion.

"You set upon three completely defenceless men and attacked them by throwing stones. The sole offence these men had committed, or so it seemed in their minds, was their colour and race.

"This sort of anti-racial behaviour does England no good at all, and I am sure you will be greatly ashamed of what you did for as long as you live."

B—— R——, aged 17, of New Barn Lane, Rochdale, was jailed for three years after being convicted by a jury of causing grievous bodily harm with intent to Mr Afzal Bux.

Six other youths admitted causing an affray.

M—— F——, aged 17, of St Martin's Street, Castleton; M—— H——, aged 17, of Kirkway, Kirkholt; S—— M——, aged 19, of Datchett Terrace, Kirkholt, and P—— S——, aged 17, of Castleway, Castleton, were each given a six-month sentence suspended for two years and were each fined £50.

L—— R——, aged 16, of Worcester Street, Rochdale, was fined £50 and S—— J——, aged 15, of Shirley Street, Castleton, was given a conditional discharge for two years.

A—— R——, aged 17, also of Worcester Street, Rochdale, was convicted by a jury of causing an affray and was given a six-month sentence suspended for two years.

F——, H——, M——, S—— and L—— R—— were each ordered to pay £50 compensation.

Mr Geoffrey Voss, prosecuting, said that on 13 July Mr Bux, of Exford, Ashfield Valley, was driving along the Ashfield Valley service road with two friends when he saw a group of girls and the defendants.

"He thought the girls were being subjected to attentions which were unwelcome and stopped the car to ask the girls if they were all right," Counsel said.

One girl told him to go away, and stones were thrown by the defendants towards Mr Bux and his car.

Mr Bux and his passengers got out of the car and the defendants ran to a canal bridge where there was a pile of bricks.

Bricks were then thrown at the three men, who turned and ran back to where the trouble had first started.

Mr Bux got into his car and drove towards the defendants. R—— then picked up a piece of pipe and threw it through the windscreen of the car, hitting Mr Bux on the head and fracturing his skull.

"Mr Bux lost consciousness and the car continued across a pavement and crashed into two garages," Mr Voss said.

Judge Bailey ordered that £100 of the compensation should be paid to Mr Bux for the damage to his car and £150 to Rochdale Corporation for damage to the garages.

Rochdale Observer, 9 March 1974

LICENSEE ACCUSED — Licensee of the Ship Inn, Milnrow Road, Rochdale, J—— P—— G—— was accused of selling alcohol to a fifteen-year-old girl and the case was adjourned until 20 March.

BREAK-IN

DOLL THOUGHT THAT SOMEBODY WAS TRYING TO BATTER the door down and when she went to find out what was going on, discovered Kenny on the step, white-faced and with his hair plastered to his head. It looked to Doll as though he might have been crying.

"What's up?" she said, fearing that something had gone wrong in the family. Kenny came in and went straight through to the kitchen, leaving a trail of wet bootprints on the composition floor. Jimmy was sitting down to his tea; considering that the pubs had been open for an hour or more this was something approaching a minor miracle. Neither the man nor the boy said a word: Kenny flopped into the chair with the broken arm and stared into the fire.

"Kenny?" Doll said tentatively. Even now she couldn't altogether resist a hesitant smile, her perfect set of teeth on display like a specimen in a dental training school.

"The old man twamped me," Kenny said into his chest. His voice was gruff and he released a long shuddering sigh.

"What for this time?" Doll said carefully; she didn't want the lad to break down and cry.

"How should I know? He came in after work and went bloody mad. The usual caper. I can't do anything now without him picking on me."

"What about your mam?"

"What about her?"

"Didn't she say anything?"

"Nowt much she could say, what with him ranting and raving." He added in an undertone and with deep, bitter feeling, "I'll get me own back."

"It must have been for something, Kenny."

It had been, of course, about money—or, more precisely, the lack of it. He had arranged with Janice to go to the Seven Stars in Heywood and had asked the old lady for a couple of quid: she had been in the kitchen cooking the tea and had pointed silently and furiously at the living-room where Brian was watching the northern news. But Brian wasn't watching the northern news: at that precise moment he was on his way to the kitchen and had caught her in the act, caught her mouthing and gesturing, and things had taken their course. Brian's anger had been held in abeyance over Christmas (a friendly gesture in the spirit of peace and goodwill towards all mankind). Kenny had been misled by the temporary truce and lapsed into his old careless ways. Instead of staying in his room and avoiding his father as much as possible, he lounged in front of the television all night, smoking his mother's cigarettes and drinking canned beer out of the fridge.

He no longer kept up the pretence of looking for a job but lay in bed till dinner-time and after egg, bacon and fried bread wandered round the flat in his mauve underpants until late afternoon. Brian didn't know about this, but he suspected it. And what really annoyed him, angered him to the point of incoherent rage, was Kenny's attitude. In the army they had called it dumb insolence, and Kenny had perfected the technique to a fine art. He would stand and stare with his slightly bulging eyes and take everything that was hurled at him without batting an eyelid or uttering a word. It was as though Brian were attempting to communicate with a deaf and dumb person, or an imbecile, or the wall.

So when he came upon the secret, silent conversation between mother and son the last shred of reason and tolerance snapped — like a steel wire under tremendous pressure — and he went at them both until Margaret, the first to give way, said, "Yes. Yes. All right. He was asking for money. He's taking Janice out and he wants a couple of quid. Is that it? Are you satisfied?" She turned off the heat under the liver and onions and pushed Brian aside to get into the living-room.

Then the fight started. Brian clipped Kenny on the ear and Kenny, who normally only defended himself, retaliated. Then Brian went berserk and leathered him. He was smaller and weighed less than Kenny but it was no contest. The liver and onions went flying and the sliding glass door in the wall cupboard was shattered. Kenny couldn't get out and ended up scriking.

"It must have been for something," Doll said, taking the dirty dishes to the sink.

"It weren't for anything."

"Money," Jimmy Mangan said.

"He's been on at me for ages," Kenny said. "I can't do anything right. He even gets mad if I take Janice home. You don't know what he's like at times; he's like a madman."

"He always was a bit too bloody handy with his fists, yon bugger," Jimmy said. He lit a Park Drive and propped his bare elbows on the table. Pale streaks showed through the grime on his arms where rivulets of soapy water had run down. He dragged the smoke into his lungs and said, "You're not on the cadge, are you?" Doll gave him a look and put her hand on Kenny's shoulder:

"Do you want a drink, love?"

"What have you got?"

"Only tea or coffee."

"Never mind." There was a catch in his voice and he was full of self-pity. It even hurt him that they didn't have any beer for him to drink. Life, it seemed, was conspiring to crush him: nobody really cared anything for him: he was all alone in the world. The flames in front of his eyes suddenly went distorted and streaky, like sunshine seen through a rainy windowpane, and he had to tense his muscles in his throat to hold back the tears.

Jimmy Mangan said, "Have you got a job yet?" and Kenny shook his head without looking up; he thought furiously: You've got fucking room to talk. "There you are then," Jimmy said. "You can't expect him to keep on forking out when you're on the dole."

"I'm not on the dole," Kenny said. "I was given the push, so I can't draw."

"There you are then." There was a silence in which Jimmy picked up his pint mug and slurped his tea. The sound reminded Kenny of a pig with its snout in the trough and he nearly lost control. He thought seriously—for just a moment—of hitting the silly old fart on the head and taking his money.

In the hallway on his way out Doll put a finger to her lips and pressed a pound note into his hand, saying loudly, "See you again, Kenny love. Give me love to your mam." She opened the front door and waved him on. "Ta-ra now." Her teeth flashed like a beacon in a dark world as Kenny went out into the rain.

. . .

The Seven Stars was fairly quiet—it was only to be expected— this being the first Friday after the New Year when most people had spent up and were short of cash. Janice knew that Kenny was in a black mood as soon as they met: his jaw was set and he didn't say a word all the way to Heywood on the bus. The rain continued to pelt down and they were both soaked by the time they got to the pub. It was a disco place and at weekends had a local group on: three or four lads who worked during the day and played for a few quid and free beer at nights—attracting the sixteen to twenties from Rochdale, Bury, and from Heywood itself.

Some of the lads were there: Crabby, Arthur, Fester and Shortarse. Kenny ignored them and sat in the corner farthest away from the long curving bar with the leatherette trim which took up all of one wall. Janice sipped her half of mild and watched the girls on the small scarred dance-floor, accustomed now to Kenny's moods and wise in the ways of dealing with them; he would come round sooner or later, and even if he didn't, anything she might say would only make matters worse.

"How's your mam?" Kenny said after ten minutes of brooding silence.

"All right. She's gone away for the weekend."

"Oh aye." He lifted his pint and the liquid was almost sucked out of the glass. "She's all right, your mam," he said, testing her.

"Yeh," Janice said non-commitally.

"Where's she gone?"

"Blackpool."

"At this time of year?"

"She has a friend there."

"Oh aye," Kenny said.

The group came on and all further conversation was curtailed to shouted observations and monosyllabic remarks. The group went through their limited repertoire of outdated top thirty hits and rock n' roll standards; Janice wanted to dance but as she knew Kenny wouldn't, had to be content to sit and listen, tapping her foot and moving her little round bottom on the seat. When he went to the bar to get more drinks Kenny was approached by Fester, who laid a fat square hand on his shoulder.

"Crabby says Skush got the chop."

"Yeh." Kenny watched him from beneath heavy eyelids and then shifted his gaze, like somebody ill-at-ease who awkwardly transfers weight from one foot to another. He said, "Did Andy tell you?"

"He told Crabby."

"He was stoned. We tried to get him away but the law arrived. There must have been ten of them."

"Did he have any stuff on him?"

"Pockets full of it."

"Fuckinell," Fester said. "Will he grass?"

The word sent a thrill through Kenny. He suddenly felt bigger and tougher and more dangerous, and life expanded within him: after all it was possession of drugs—a criminal offence—and the law was involved. "Skush isn't a nark," he said, matching Fester's word with one of his own.

"They're bastards though; they could trick him into telling them your name and Andy's. You want to get an alibi or get away for a bit."

"Yeh," Kenny said thoughtfully. He was thrilled at the idea, but at the same time felt a slight unease. And yet he wasn't afraid, not truly afraid: the real and actual possibility of being picked up by the police was something that happened to other people, like getting cancer, or being run over by a bus. They might get Skush, they might get Andy, but they'd never get him.

"Hello stranger," a girl's voice said, and it was Eileen from Woolworth's.

"What are you doing in a duff place like this?" Kenny asked.

"Same as you."

She still had the blatant, unabashed stare that both discomfited and excited him. A picture flashed instantaneously through his mind of her lying back with her legs open, inviting him to have it away. She would be that kind of girl: straight in, first time, no messing. He remembered a girl (but not her name) who had invited him into her house during the school holidays and they had lain on her mother's cerise eiderdown and it had taken what seemed like hours to unfasten her bra, finally, at long last, revealing little pink rosebud nipples which he hadn't known what to do with and could only gaze at in dumbstruck awe. It was the first time he had been overcome by such intense sexual excitement, and Eileen evoked the same response — he couldn't get his breath properly and was shaken by an almost uncontrollable desire to reach out in the crowded pub and grab her breasts.

"On your own?" Eileen said, moving in next to him. (Fester had raised his eyebrows, pursed his lips, and gone.)

"No, I've got a bird with me."

"Regular girlfriend eh?"

"Not really." Kenny let his eyelids droop. "She hangs around a bit. What can you do?" They looked into each other's eyes. "How's Woolies these days?"

"Same. Irwin's always on your back. As usual."

"That twat. He wants fucking strangling, that cunt."

"Yeh. He's a right cunt," Eileen said deliberately, her eyes locked on his. Kenny's hands were perspiring. Why had he never got to grips with it when he had a chance? He knew she would go like a rattlesnake and here it was staring him in the face and he couldn't do a thing about it. Apart from kicking Janice into touch.

"Do you fancy a trip to Luton?" he said straight out of the blue. Eileen's mouth curved in a small mocking smile. Kenny lowered his voice as though somebody might be eavesdropping. "They're playing the Dale in a couple of weeks and I'm going down on the coach. Fancy it?"

"Yeh," Eileen said. "Why not?"

"I'll see you in Woolies," Kenny said. "I'll come in one afternoon and fix it up."

"Yeh." She was still watching him as he turned to go; Kenny was unnerved. He got back to the table with the drinks and when he looked up she was smiling at him over her shoulder.

"Who's that?"

"Who?"

"That girl."

"Who wants to know?"

"I only asked who she was," Janice said plaintively.

"Somebody I used to work with."

"Have you ever taken her out?"

"What?" Kenny said. "No." And then remembering himself, "What's it to you? What if I have? So what?" He was thrusting his face near hers, wanting to hurt her, to make her cry. He gripped the flesh of her forearm between his bitten fingers and pressed it as hard as he could till all the blood had gone, leaving an area of tiny blue bruise-marks. When she cried out he thumped her on the muscle of the upper arm and kept repeating, "Shut up. Shut up."

Even when they got outside and were walking towards the chip shop on the main road there was too much violent energy in him that had yet to be dissipated. They walked apart, Kenny scuffing his boots on the pavement and Janice desolate and in tears. She loved him and was afraid of him: she couldn't understand what drove him. Why did he want to hurt her? What was so wrong with the world that he had to inflict pain on other people — like a spiteful, obstinate child that must smash and destroy everything around it?

Inside the fluorescent brightness and greasy warmth of the chip shop they stood in line, not touching, and waited their turn at the high stainless steel counter. The man was scooping sizzling brown fish out of the hot fat. Kenny didn't even bother to ask Janice what she wanted; she noticed that he couldn't take his eyes off a boy in front of them in the queue — a young man, rather, in a midnight-blue velvet suit with flared trousers. His hands were white and nicely-kept, with long tapering fingers, and his hair had obviously been washed, trimmed and blow-waved at one of those boutique-type hairdressers, probably in Manchester. At the kerb was a low-slung sports job—a Lotus—and the blonde hair of a girl splayed over the back of the leather seat.

As he was going out with his order Kenny sniggered down his nose and the young man half-turned and went on. Janice was prepared for something to happen but nothing did. She prayed that the car would drive away: the mood Kenny was in, the venom spurting inside him, could lead only to damage, either to property or people.

The car was still there when they came out. Janice tried to stay close to him, clutching his arm, but he shook her off. He stood in the middle of the pavement, his eyes hooded, eating fish and chips, and said in a loud voice: "Hey, Jan. What kind of a ponce would buy a shit-heap of a car like this?"

As expected, there was no response. Kenny continued to watch the young man through the windscreen. The blonde girl was saying something to him, and, although they couldn't hear her, obviously in a low voice.

"It must be a ponce," Kenny said loudly to Janice. "A fairy. Look how shiny it is. I bet he polishes it a lot. Or gets his mummy to do it for him."

The young man wanted to drive away; the girl was begging him to drive away; but for that reason he couldn't. Kenny tossed a greasy chip on to the shiny bonnet. Janice shrank away into the shadow. The car door opened and the young man got out.

"Watch what you're doing," he said.

Kenny stopped eating. His jaw went stiff. "Are you talking to me?" he said.

"Just watch the car, that's all."

"Or what?" And when the young man didn't answer, "Or what will you do?"

It was coming, it was coming, Janice could see it happening in front of her eyes. The badness was spilling out of him, it had to be released. If the young man didn't get in the car now it would be too late. She saw Kenny's hands with the tattooed knuckles wadding the newspaper into a tight greasy ball: she could almost sense the nervous energy vibrating in his arms: he had to take his spite and hate and frustration out on somebody.

"I don't want to argue with you, friend," the young man said. He still had one foot inside the car; he was that uncertain; and the girl was pleading with him to drive away.

Kenny said slowly, "I'm not your fucking friend." He threw the ball of newspaper on to the bonnet and stood with his arms hanging straight down at his sides. For the first time that evening, Janice realised, he was enjoying himself. His fingers were actually twitching with suppressed eagerness. A fist in the face and a boot in the bollocks were his idea of how to end a good night out.

"Kenny…" Janice said, but—as she knew he would—Kenny ignored her. And then the small miracle she had hoped for, and given up hope, happened. The young man got into the car and drove off. Kenny ran into the road and kicked at the rear bumper but missed.

All the way home on the bus he was distracted and fretful. She tried to cheer him up. "Me mum's away. I've got the key. We've got the flat to ourselves. You can stay the night."

"Great," Kenny said without enthusiasm. He wiped the window with his sleeve and stopped in mid-motion. He looked at her. "You're all electric in the flats, aren't you?" he said. Janice nodded. "And have they all got meters?"

AWAY

LUTON IS 163 MILES FROM ROCHDALE WHICH MEANS THAT the coach has to leave the town-centre by eleven o'clock at the latest. The day is wet and miserable, with the coach whipping up a funnel of spray in its wake as it heads south down the M6. In the front seats sit the staunch, respectable, middle-aged supporters who follow Rochdale's ailing progress in the Third Division out of a kind of stoic self-denial: they feel themselves to be martyrs whose redemption will come through sacrifice to a lost cause. In the back sit the rowdies. They see the country as divided into battle-lines — a number of isolated feudal kingdoms constantly at war with one another which send out rival bands of marauders to plunder and pillage and spread alarm amongst the citizenry. They are the spear-head of attack, infiltrating behind enemy lines, with memories of past victories to sustain them and the promise of fresh glories to come. Their scarves flap damply out of the windows and empty beer cans roll about under the seats.

Eileen sits in the corner window seat next to Kenny; the bumpy coach ride is making him randy and once or twice he has clumsily attempted to put his hand on her knee but Eileen has rebuffed him with an ease that is almost patronising. She seems to possess a vast amount of knowledge about life which unsettles Kenny and somehow makes him feel inadequate. Janice he can handle — no problem — and the lads don't worry him either (with them it's a matter of bluff and double-bluff, beating them down with a word, a look, a gesture) but with Eileen he gets the impression that she can see right through him and has the uncomfortable feeling that she might even be laughing at him. She has what he considers to be a very sexy mouth: her teeth are large and protrude slightly, making her lips permanently moist and available. Her flat open stare takes everything in, cool, withdrawn and yet watchful, as if the world passing before her eyes contains nothing that would surprise or alarm her. She has it all weighed up, Kenny decides, and he doesn't know whether he likes it.

"What about your girlfriend?"

"Who says she's my girlfriend?" Kenny says predictably. He will never admit to anything, especially the truth.

"You were with her that night."

"Yeh. Well..." he shrugs unconvincingly, "...she's just a bird, that's all." And then adds mysteriously: "She was useful to me."

Eileen turns away from the window to look at him. Spray fans out like steam and the tyres make a sucking noise on the tarmac. "How do you mean?"

"We pulled a job together," Kenny says, feeling the need to impress her, show her that he can play the game as well as anybody. At the same time he's alarmed at his own rashness; if you talk too much you never know where it might lead...

"You mean you stole something?"

"Yeh, sort of." He has to go on now that he's gone this far, and tells her the story of the break-in: four meters in one night: clean away without a smell of the law.

Eileen is impressed. He has her full undivided attention.

"It's better than working," Kenny boasts.

"How much did you get?"

"A few dabs."

"How much though?"

"Seventeen quid."

"Seventy?"

"Seven*teen*."

"Out of *four* meters?"

"We'd have got more," Kenny says quickly, "only they'd just been emptied. Still, it was better than nowt."

"Didn't the police ask any questions?"

"The cops," Kenny says as though she'd made a small joke. "Yeh, they asked Janice and her mother but her mother was away for the weekend and Janice said the place must have been broken into Sunday afternoon because everything was all right till then."

"I thought you said Friday night."

"We did the meters on Friday night," Kenny says, lowering his voice, "but Jan told the police it was Sunday because that's when the new lodger was due to arrive. What we did was to break in the other three flats—except his—so they'd think it was him. We opened his door with the key and just did the meter. On the others we broke the locks as well."

Eileen thinks this out and says admiringly, "You planned it all."

"Yeh, course I did," Kenny says, lighting a cigarette and sinking back in the seat.

"They suspected the lodger instead of you."

"Right."

"So they got him instead."

"No," Kenny says. "He never showed up. He's still in Shrewsbury."

. . .

After the match—which the visiting team lose 2–1—Kenny and some of the Rochdale supporters go on a tiny rampage through the streets of Luton. It has to be tiny: there are only eight of them, Eileen and another girl included. At one point they are chased by a dozen-or-so Luton supporters and lose their way, and by the time they get back to the ground the car park is deserted: the coach has gone. It is dark and cold, although the rain has stopped.

Kenny, unblooded so far that day, leads the way to the nearest pub and they sit among the early drinkers feeding themselves with crisps, cheese snacks and cold meat pies. One of the lads says,

"What are we going to do now?"

"No use moaning," Kenny says. "We've missed it and that's that."

"I'm not moaning; I'm just saying what are we going to do now? We've nowhere to kip."

"For Christ's sake stop worrying. You get on my bleeding nerves."

"I'm not worrying. I just said——"

"All right. Forget it."

"How are we going to get back?" Eileen says. She asks the question out of interest, not in the least anxious or perturbed, and Kenny admires her for it.

"Thumb it."

"Tonight?"

"No, tomorrow."

"But what about tonight?"

"We'll be all right," Kenny says, holding her eyes with his own. She meets his look openly, on equal terms, without a trace of archness. He wonders what it is going to be like when his mouth is pressing against her open wet lips, his tongue working away behind her protruding teeth — anticipating the experience with a kind of scared lust.

Fortunately, between the eight of them, there is enough money to buy beer for the evening and by eight-thirty they are all merry and slightly bored. They are in a strange town, among people who speak with an unfamiliar accent, and the possibilities are endless: it is simply a matter of deciding on a course of action which promises the most thrills. Even roaming the streets is exhilarating because every corner brings a new and unexpected landscape; everything is so different from their northern industrial experience that the air itself seems charged with mystery and danger.

They try several pubs, working their way towards the centre of town. Kenny can't get used to the beer, which seems thick and dark and slightly sweet-tasting: northern beer is lighter with a sharper edge to it. He walks with his arm around Eileen's waist and hers around his, now and then catching a passing whiff of her smell whose strangeness and unfamiliarity makes him conscious that beneath her clothes is an unknown body, with its dark recesses and secret places.

"I hope they don't catch you," Eileen says.

"Who's that?"

"The police."

He gives her a sidelong glance. "Do you reckon they will?"

"I don't know," Eileen says. "Anyway, you can always say you were with me."

This is one of the nicest things anyone has ever said to Kenny. That—and the beer—fills his stomach with a rosy warmth. He hugs her to him as they walk along and then says in a low voice so the others can't hear, "I fancied you a lot when I worked at Woolies."

"You never said owt."

"We don't where I come from."

"I fancied you," Eileen says after a slight pause.

This is Kenny's cue to slip his hand inside her coat and squeeze her breast. She makes a sound, a moan that is almost inaudible, which thrills Kenny down to his boots. He feels the tug of a gathering erection.

Much of the bravado seems to leave the group after the pubs shut at eleven, though the hard reality of a cold night ahead with nowhere to sleep is disoriented by the beer swimming in their heads: it is an inarticulate fear hovering just out of reach outside the periphery of an alcoholic haze. Down a dark windy backstreet Kenny stops suddenly at the sight of a white plastic sign swinging on creaking hinges. It reads: *Liberal Club*. Two of the lads run to the street corners to keep an eye out while the others examine the door, studded with iron rivets.

"We'll never do this," one of them says.

Kenny calls them together. "Round the back. Try the windows." Eileen goes with Kenny and helps him shin up to a window with a long vertical rectangular fanlight. He stands on her shoulders to reach the ledge, scrabbling in the darkness for a handhold, and grips the lower edge of the fanlight which stands proud of the main window. He feels along it, standing with the toes of his boots on the ledge and his arms outstretched overhead, hoping to find a catch or a projection of some kind which he can use as a point of leverage. There isn't one. He curses and in a fit of temper pulls at the lower edge of the fanlight, which swings open and upwards without a sound. The abruptness of it, the silence — and the shock — nearly send him off-balance, and for a moment he hovers on the toes of his boots before grabbing the frame of the open window and hauling himself upright.

"What's wrong?" Eileen says, alarmed at the flurry of movement above her.

"I've fucking done it!" Kenny whispers, "get the others."

"Fucking great!" Eileen says.

Kenny wants to shout in jubilation. The bastards can knock him down as much as they want to but Kenny Seddon always has the last laugh. It's easy to beat the system: a doddle — a meter here, a break-in there, a girlfriend at home and a fast bird away. Why work and sweat when the world lies defenceless before you, begging to be plundered and fucked and made to look a prize tool?

The first thing the lads do is help themselves to drinks at the bar. The pumps are working and it's pints all round. Kenny opens the cash-register but it's too much to hope for that he will find any money; in fact there's a handful of one and two-pence pieces.

One of the lads says, "Find summat to eat, I'm starving."

"What is there? Look in that tin."

"Crisps."

"Is that all?"

"Salted peanuts."

"Shit, look at all these fags. Kenny!"

"Keep it down, for fuck's sake," Kenny says. "Take what you want but pipe down."

They guzzle several pints of beer each and then start on shorts. Glasses are smashed and bodies crash about in the gloomy depths of the hall, footsteps thumping on the bare dusty boards. Somebody puts money into the black meter on the wall and the oblong canopy hanging on grimy chains from the ceiling floods the billiard table in a blaze of vivid green. The lads grab cues from the rack and empty the wooden box of snooker balls onto the table. At first there is an attempt at a sensible, orderly game but before long it's a free-for-all with everyone cracking away at whatever comes within range. They start acting the fool, hitting the balls harder and harder, until inevitably somebody mis-cues and rips a long ragged gash in the smooth green baize. It makes a sound like somebody farting. Eileen falls against Kenny, laughing helplessly, and the glass of neat rum slips from her fingers and shatters on the floor.

Kenny too is drunk, but not drunk enough not to know what he wants. The ripping and smashing goes on while he pulls her through a door behind the bar and into a room with crates stacked against the walls and brown cartons of Golden Wonder crisps piled on top of one another: the pale rectangular window gives enough light to make out a row of varnished light switches and a cheap calendar reproduction of Windsor Castle (with the Queen not at home). They stumble about amidst the dim clutter, trying to lend each other support and at the same time hang on.

"Here," Eileen says, "down here."

Kenny thinks she means the cellar but she means down on the floor in the corner where there's a pile of sacking, discarded packaging and old display cards advertising Babycham. The strong beery smell in the small room is mingled faintly with that of disinfectant; paper and cellophane crackle under their weight as they collapse into it, befuddled, unco-ordinated; and Kenny can't help laughing at the thought that they'll both end up smelling like a brewery.

Eileen's wet mouth fastens to his and stops both laughter and thought: her coat is open and she wraps her legs round the back of his. There is something desperate in her kisses, a blind insatiable seeking like that of a burrowing creature anxious to hide away from the daylight. Composure has gone: the mask of cool self-possession replaced by shut eyes and hot urging mouth. Kenny is hard and randy, but he wants to pee. The lump is painful in his trousers, part erection and part pissproud. He gropes for her breasts, encounters their soft rise and fall beneath the material of her dress, and Eileen makes a guttural noise which vibrates against his gums. She wrenches her mouth away and reaches below.

"Is it out?"

"What?" Kenny says, taken aback.

"Get it out ... I want it, I want it."

Her hands are at his belt, unfastening the buckle and drawing the end through the loops. She unzips him and Kenny feels the rush of cold air between his legs and then the luxurious sense of release as it uncoils itself from its cramped hiding place and stands up at full stretch, giving off heat and a delicate but unmistakable odour.

"Fucking hell," Eileen whispers, taking hold.

Kenny has never been appreciated in this way before; it brings him quickly to the boil so that he wants to get on with the job without further delay. But Eileen is in control of the situation: she is like a greedy little girl who can't wait to get at the chocolate eclairs but knows the feast will be all the more enjoyable if only she can be patient.

"Isn't it nice," she says in a breath, holding on to him. "And big."

"You're fantastic," Kenny tells her.

"I love it. I love holding it. I bet it feels great sticking up hard. Does it feel great?"

"Yeh."

"Do you like me holding it? What do you like best: if I hold it or work it up and down like this?"

"I don't really mind," Kenny says breathing in and out slowly. He can't believe what is happening is actually happening. He's heard about girls like this but didn't credit the stories as being true. The tension is too much: he is nearly coming: he says, "Go easy, kid. Bloody hell. Jesus. You're fantastic."

Eileen smiles at him in the darkened corner, the weak light from the window shining on her protruding teeth and wet lips. She moves below and encircles him with her mouth, her head moving rhythmically up and down, her hair brushing the insides of his thighs. Kenny lies back amongst the waste paper and cellophane wrappings, lost to the world, the focal point of his existence concentrated on the incredible smooth sliding hotness.

He is nearly at the point of no return and has to stop her before it is too late. Eileen raises her head and brings her open sticky mouth down on his. They fight each other with their tongues, their lips snarling in silent rage. Eileen frees herself from her clothing and murmurs in his ear, "Do it to me. Go on, Kenny, do it."

He thinks he understands her but he doesn't — until she pushes his head lower and lower, past her breasts and the bunched clothing at her waist to the warm furry place which is prickly against his cheeks. Tentatively he pokes about, inhaling the heavy intoxicating smell, caught between the two conflicting emotions that if he doesn't fuck her right this minute he will have to go for a piss.

Eileen begins to moan and move her legs, then starts to gasp like a distance runner on the final sprint; her breathing is hoarse, shocked, between ecstasy and a cry for help, and just when Kenny is debating the next move grips him by the hair and one ear and hauls him up to lie full-length on top of her. In a moment—a mad jerking panic—it is all over. The tension is released, the iron weight in his belly turns into a balloon, and apart from wanting badly to urinate he feels quite peaceful.

"Do you think we'll get back all right?" Eileen asks, pulling her tights up.

"We'll thumb it," Kenny says, disentangling his underpants from his boots. "I've done it before. If we start off early we should be home by teatime."

"All the lot of us?"

"We'll split up. You and me together and the rest of them in ones and twos."

The cellophane crackles as Eileen stands up and smoothes the wrinkles from her dress. "I'm starving."

"I'm a bit peckish," Kenny admits, "but first I need a piss." He gets up and then goes quite still; he stands listening and waves his hand to stop Eileen rummaging in the waste paper for her shoes.

"What's up?" Eileen says, her voice hushed by the way he waits silently in the darkness, the pale light outlining his head and shoulders in an attitude of frozen concentration. She listens also but can hear nothing. It occurs to her that it shouldn't be this quiet, unless, that is, the others are asleep or have gone away.

For some reason best known to himself Kenny is moving stealthily towards the door, placing the toe of each boot carefully before the next, and very slowly opens it the merest fraction so that a thin crack of yellow appears: Eileen can hear the low murmur of voices and smiles with relief. For a moment a dozen foolish notions had passed through her mind—the others had gone and left them, or the police had noticed the light and crept in to make an arrest, or——

Kenny hasn't moved and is intent on watching something. And then she sees him put his hand in his pocket and take out an object which catches the light.

. . .

The reason they hadn't heard anything was that the others were kettled and didn't realise what was happening until it was too late. When it had happened they stood blearily with their backs to the billiard table, wondering in their stupor how it was possible for seven people to get into the hall without being seen or heard. Kenny, on all fours behind the bar, his heart thumping in his chest, listens to what is being said. There hasn't been a fight yet (he would have heard it in the small back room) but it's shaping up nicely to a barney with what the Luton lads reckon are good odds: seven against five, not counting the girl. Kenny has weighed them up through the crack in the door: two of them are big bastards, six footers at least, a couple of real tough nuts wearing short leather jackets studded in fancy metal scrolls enclosing the names 'Johnny' and 'Sugar'—topple these two, Kenny knows, and the rest are a bag of shite tied in the middle with string. One of the others is a nig-nog in a blue and white bob-cap, short, stocky, with a squat ugly face and the makings of a scrubby beard; the remaining four are a nondescript ragbag of townies who look as though they couldn't raise a decent wank between them.

It's one of the big lads doing all the talking and Kenny bides his time. He's not daft enough to stick his neck out before he has to— and in any case the Luton mob will soon start something or one of his own mates will grab a billiard cue and splinter it over the head of one of the leather jackets.

"What are you doing down here then?" the big lad is saying. He has a terrible complexion. Kenny knows this kind of talk well: it is the gentle deception before the onslaught, the friendly gesture before the fist in the teeth. Answer them back, Kenny thinks, don't let them scare you.

"Town were playing pathetic Rochdale today," says one of the nondescript ragbags.

"Do they play football up there?" says the big lad. "Do they? Well. I thought they didn't have any grass to play on up there. What do they play in then — clogs and flat caps?"

"We're not a load of pansies at any rate."

The big lad says, "Rate?" twisting his face and pronouncing it the northern way. "Raaate. What does raaate mean?" The others laugh. "Why don't you talk proper instead of talking stupid?"

"They're not civilised north of Coventry, Johnny."

"It's a shame you don't understand us," one of the Rochdale lads says. "You big dozy cunt."

"Take that back," the big lad says swiftly, no longer sweetness and light. "I said: Take it back."

"I thought you didn't know what we were on about. You southern pouf."

The odd thing about violence is that it comes so suddenly and happens so quickly that it doesn't seem real at all: the reality is delayed, like a bomb operated by a time-switch, ticking, deadly, with the devastation yet to come. In the hall with the hooded light it strikes with the swiftness of a venomous snake, happening here and now in front of everyone's eyes — yet finding them static, unprepared, wetting their pants.

After that opening incident Kenny lives through a bad moment when his legs won't seem to move. It's like a dream when your feet get stuck in treacle and it comes as a surprise when he finds himself on the other side of the bar swinging a bottle and running, actually running, at one of the leather jackets. There are three bodies on the billiard table, each body fighting the other two. Kenny is annoyed and distracted by this and pauses to crack the head that doesn't seem familiar, and hopes, in the rush, he hasn't made a mistake. When he goes on the leather jacket he had in mind has disappeared and he has to seek a fresh target: the ugly nig-nog in the bob-cap who is kicking something along the floor, a sack, or a cat, or perhaps a human being.

"Nigger," Kenny says into his black ear and as the boy turns— he is about fourteen, Kenny sees, with odd-coloured eyes—smashes the bottle across the bridge of his nose and the bottle does something he has seen in movies but never before in real life: it actually breaks.

There is an instant mess of splinters and blood, a brilliant gash with the nose laid open to the bone, amid gobs of red stuff flying in all directions. The result is so spectacular that for a moment Kenny is lost in dreadful contemplation, a little awestruck by his own handiwork. He steps back in wonder and is taken hold of by the throat and his spine rammed against the edge of the billiard table, bent backwards at a terrible angle, the light hitting him in the eyes and somewhere on the edge of his vision the smooth brown butt of a billiard cue sliding—or is it swinging?—coming at his head. He twists left and feels the impact rattle the coloured balls and vibrate through the table to his skull. Kenny is amazed. He has never met anyone with the strength to pin him down with one hand and strike with the other.

He thinks ... he is about to think when he sees the butt coming again and three things happen simultaneously: urine runs down his leg and the black meter on the wall clicks and the light goes out. For an instant—it can be no more—everything stops: blackness and silence cover everything, and when it is over Kenny is thankful that he can withdraw the knife blade as silently and unobtrusively as it went in.

POLICE

THE BEGINNING OF THE END WAS AT HAND FOR KENNY Seddon. On the 25th of January (a week before his seventeenth birthday) WPC T——, the local Juvenile Liaison Officer, paid a visit to the flat and asked why he hadn't reported the Friday before to the Rochdale Police headquarters. Kenny told her he had been ill with stomach trouble, and Miss T—— asked who his doctor was.

"I didn't bother going to the doctor," Kenny said. "I just stayed in bed. I've had it before; it's nowt serious."

"Next time get a doctor's note. You know you can get into serious trouble if you fail to report when you're supposed to."

"Yeh," Kenny said. "I'll remember that." He looked into her face. "Do you want a cup of tea?"

"No thank you. Did you hear what I said?"

"Yeh. I'll remember, don't worry." He tucked his vest into his jeans and flopped down on the settee. He was okay now but it had been a bad moment when he had opened the door and seen her standing there—his heart had lurched and he had felt his face going red. Even as she followed him down the dark staircase he had had the sense of terror that this was it, had actually expected her opening sentence to contain the words 'Luton' and 'knifing' and 'arrest'. But now it was fine: he was relaxed: nothing could touch him.

Miss T—— said, "*I'm* not worried, Kenneth. It's up to you, it's your look-out." Her eyes were hard but she couldn't hold his gaze for long and glanced round the flat at the discarded clothing on the chairs and the empty mug and breakfast plate on the floor. There were crumbs on the settee where Kenny lay sprawled.

"See you," Kenny said as she prepared to leave.

Miss T—— stopped at the door. "I thought you were going to try and get a job? Have you done anything about it?"

"I've been looking in the *Observer*," Kenny lied smoothly. "There is nowt though."

"You don't call that really trying, do you?"

"What else can I do?"

"Go to the Youth Employment near the station. Tell them what kind of job you'd like and they'll send you a postcard if anything comes along that would suit you. You've worked in engineering haven't you?"

"Yeh," Kenny said indifferently.

"Well then: put your name down."

"I don't really fancy doing that again."

"What job do you fancy?"

"Millionaire's pig," Kenny said, watching her lazily.

"Don't be silly, Kenneth," Miss T—— said. "How do you expect to stay out of trouble if you don't have a job?"

"There's nowt I fancy doing. I can't get a soft touch like yours, you know." He lit a cigarette and crossed his arms behind his head; Miss T—— looked at his hairy armpits and quickly turned away, almost imagining she could smell the unwashed sweat.

"I want to hear that you've put your name down the next time I see you," she said curtly. "That'll be on the 15th of February."

"I'll be there," Kenny said. "You can find your own way out, can't you?"

When he heard the front door close he had a quiet snigger to himself, lying back with the smoke drifting past his eyes, wriggling his toes in the stiff wrinkled socks. There was no need to get alarmed; no need at all. If they had anything on him they'd have picked him up days ago. It had even made the national newspapers (he still had the cutting from the *Mirror*)—which had given him a shock at first, he had to admit, the big black headline on page three and underneath it the story of the 'Luton gangfight' in which a lad had to be rushed to hospital and given an emergency transfusion. It was all over now, he kept telling himself, blood under the bridge. Yet still he had to be careful, to keep a check on what he said: the trouble was that he found himself wanting to tell people—even strangers—that Kenny Seddon had knifed somebody in a gang-fight. He got a thrill whenever he thought about it—a terrifying thrill that crawled up inside his belly and stuck fast in his throat. He wanted to say, "Do you know who you're talking to? I knifed a bloke. It was in the paper."

The rest of the afternoon he sat watching *Crown Court*, *Play School* and *Magpie* on television, smoking the last of the cigarettes he had nicked from the Liberal Club, eating salted peanuts and picking the hard skin off the soles of his feet. Kat came in at ten-past four and made him a mug of instant coffee sweetened with three spoonfuls of condensed milk; then Margaret appeared and without a word dumped her bag on the chair and went into the kitchen to make the tea. Brian usually came home at five-thirty and at twenty minutes past Kenny shoved his socks into his pocket and went to his room. He couldn't stand to be in the same room as Brian. The air seemed to be charged with negative particles of hate. They would enter and leave the room without looking at one another, circling the furniture with their eyes carefully averted and making it clear that when they spoke it was to the other members of the family.

Kenny waited till the others had finished eating and then had his tea in the kitchen alone. By seven-thirty he was clomping along the concrete walkways in the direction of the Weavers. There was a thin scattering of snow over the Estate, scooped into corners by the wind and lying like icing sugar on the frozen puddles. He didn't stay long there, had a swift pint and carried on under the railway viaduct and up New Barn Lane to the new bypass which linked Rochdale to the M62. The traffic whipped by in an icy blast, the red tail-lights streaking along the dual carriageway to the roundabout at the junction of Half Acre and the motorway access road.

Kenny was undecided what to do: whether to walk up to Janice's or catch the bus to town. It was early for the lads to be about but at the same time he didn't feel like traipsing all the way up Bury Road. And ever since the break-in he had kept away from the flat as much as possible; he somehow felt safer at a distance. The cold wind made the rims of his ears sting and he hunched himself in the corner of the bus shelter to conserve as much warmth as he could inside the thin shirt and flimsy jacket. The cars went past in an endless procession. All the rich bastards, Kenny reflected, safe and snug behind the curved glass with the dashboard illuminating the lower parts of their smug faces. Get them out here though, in the freezing cold, away from their cars, and they were frightened, timid, spineless. Not one of them would have a notion what to do against a boot or a sharpened spindle or a fistful of steel washers. The real world belonged to him; theirs was confined to the semi-detached bungalow behind its tidy lawn and a few choice pubs which catered for passing trade—and in-between, *his* territory, the night-time streets, which they could cross only in the sealed comfort and security of steel and glass and moulded rubber trim. He shouted something and laughed, and the laughter sounded hollow and bounced back in his face from the walls and ceiling of the shelter.

The town itself was barely alive at this hour, but with each bus-load from the districts the crowds multiplied and grew, the tempo building up as the bars got full and the bingo halls prepared for the first session of eyes down, look in. As the bus swayed along the Esplanade Kenny ran full tilt down the metal stairs and jumped off as the automatic doors were opening in front of the GPO. The pavements were slushy underfoot and a few flakes of snow still lingered in the cold night air, floating down under the yellow lights.

. . .

It was gone nine o'clock before Janice showed up. Kenny, Andy and a few other lads were sitting in the White Lion arguing about how many cinemas Rochdale used to have before most of them either closed down or were turned into bingo halls. Kenny said ten: Regal, Rialto, Palace, Empire, Hippodrome, Victory, Pavilion, Kings, Ceylon, and a fleapit in Castleton whose name he couldn't remember.

"You can't count that," said one of the lads Kenny hadn't met before. "We're talking about cinemas in Rochdale. And the Ceylon doesn't count either; that was up Heybrook way."

"Heybrook's still in Rochdale, you dozy pillock," Kenny said.

"It's not in the centre though."

"I know it's not in the centre but it's still Rochdale, innit? We're talking about cinemas in *Rochdale*." He put his arm round Janice as she sat down. He said, "All right, love?" feeling kindly disposed towards her. (He was in the mood for a good poke.) "Do you want half of mild?"

"Have you enough money?"

"The old lady lent me a quid. Well sort of lent it me. Here, get us a pint while you're there," giving her a fifty-pence piece.

Fester said, "How do you fancy going over to Leeds tonight?"

"What's in Leeds?" Andy said.

Fester leaned his squat elbows on the table. "All-nighter. It's a soul club Alan and Rod have been to. Great. Stacked with talent."

"It's too bloody far," Kenny said. "By the time we get the train and waste time pissing about trying to find——"

"Alan's got transport," Fester said, his tiny slitted eyes flicking

[173]

excitedly from face to face. "We can do it in an hour on the motorway. What do you think? The five of us."

"Six," Kenny said. "Including Jan."

The car was a dark-blue 1968 Ford Consul with rusty bumpers and a rear nearside spring in danger of collapse. Kenny, Janice and Andy sat in the back and Fester and Rod got in the front next to Alan.

"Is it taxed?" Kenny asked, not having seen a disc on the windscreen.

"No," Alan said, grating into first gear. "It hasn't got an MOT either."

"When did you pass your driving test?" Andy said.

"Haven't taken it yet," Alan said.

Snow was blowing horizontally across the motorway as they climbed up beyond Milnrow, crossed the Rakewood Viaduct and topped the moors into Yorkshire. It was cosy with the heater on, gazing out from the dark interior of the car at the flurries of snow being driven silently through the beams of the headlights. Kenny had his hand on Janice's thigh. Andy said to Rod:

"You've trapped off at this place, have you?"

"Yeh. Last week."

"She all right?"

"Fit as a butcher's dog." Rod was a handsome boy with long blond hair and intense brown eyes surrounded by soft dark lashes. He kept glancing at Janice, Kenny noticed, no doubt he fancied his chances; if only he knew that just a few days ago Kenny had knifed a bloke for less. But then some of these turds always had to push their luck until it was too late.

When they got there the club turned out to be a bit of a dump. The bar consisted of three trestle tables in the shape of a U and there was no draught beer or lager, only bottles and shorts.

"Worse than fucking Chorley," Fester complained. Nearly everybody was high on something, mostly pills, and by midnight there were more bodies on the floor than standing upright. Many of the girls looked as if they hadn't had a wash or brushed their hair for several weeks. Kenny was proud of Janice: compared to the slags she was a contender for Miss United Kingdom.

She said, "Me mum wasn't for letting me come out tonight."

"Why, what's up?"

"She's still mad about the meters."

"Weren't your fault."

"She blames me for not reporting it sooner. She's had to pay it back to the Electricity Board."

"What, all of it?"

"Yeh."

"All seventeen quid?"

Janice nodded.

"What about the insurance? Didn't she claim off them?"

"They wouldn't pay up. They said the flats should have been looked after by a responsible person and as I'm under-age I don't count. So she's had to pay for new locks as well."

"She doesn't think ...?" Kenny said.

"No," Janice said quickly.

"Just you be careful then. Keep your mouth shut. I don't want any twat of a copper knocking on my door."

He recalled the moment of seeing the Juvenile Liaison Officer standing there and his heart moved again as though the incident had to be re-lived and wasn't safely past, over and done with. Then he thought about it rationally and the tension drained out of him: there was no way they could connect him with what had happened in Luton. Was there? He had to think very hard and when he had was almost certain there wasn't. There wasn't, was there? He had never been to Luton in his life — that was it — on 'the day in question' he had been ... with Janice? Yes, he had been with Janice all that day; they had gone to Manchester on the train. Why did you go to Manchester? We went to Manchester ... now then ... we went to Manchester, yes, to buy soul records. Bradleys in Rochdale don't stock the records we like, so Jan and me went to Manchester to buy soul records. For my birthday. Which records? Ah. (He'd better buy some new soul records just in case.) Here they are, look, the ones we bought. Okay? Satisfied?

... Anyway, calm down, he told himself, no need to get worked up. Jan would stick by him and none of the lads he'd been with would dare squeal because they knew what they'd get. They all knew he could do it. They'd all seen him knife a bloke.

Janice is snuggling against him, giving him ideas. The room is hot with bodies and yet has a dank sour smell like that of sweat gone cold. Janice closes her eyes and lifts her mouth for his kiss, blindly, her thin young face passive and trusting. He kisses her and afterwards she holds him tight and murmurs in his ear, "I'll never let you down, Kenny. Never."

Kenny is strangely moved by this and a lump fills his throat. He knows he has found the only girl for him and that whatever happens — whoever else might attract him — Jan is the one he wants to stay with. He has to have someone he can depend on in this rotten miserable world and she is the only one. The realisation of this makes him shiver, a swift tremor down his back that of all the people in the world Jan is on his side. It is a thought that brings comfort.

He hesitates for a moment and then forms the words: "I love you, Jan."

"I love you," Janice says. "Oh I do." She kisses him impulsively, in a dream of perfect happiness. She is loved by someone, loved in return by the person she loves. Everything becomes comprehensible to her, everything is clear and sharply defined as though a mystery has, in an instant, resolved itself and in so doing given her fresh eyes and a new vision of life.

On the way back (it was half-past one when they left the club) they sit holding one another, their closed eyes shutting out the dark rushing motorway and the headlights splayed out ahead. The floor of the car vibrates through their feet, with occasionally the hard jarring irritation of the failing rear spring. Andy is asleep in the corner, snoring gently.

"Do you think people should get married early—you know, young?"

"What brought this on?"

"Something me mum said."

"What, about me?"

"Well: yeh. It was to do with you."

"What did she say?"

"She asked me—I think she was having a joke—she asked me when we were getting engaged."

"Oh aye."

"Yeh. Last week."

"What did you say?"

"I didn't say owt. It's not up to me, is it?"

"Does she reckon you're old enough to get engaged?"

"Not right yet. Not now. But I'll be sixteen later this year. Loads of girls get engaged at sixteen. Some even get married."

"Aye they do. Some don't get wed till they're twenty-odd."

"Is that what you think?"

"Up to them, innit? Suits some folk to get married early and doesn't suit others. Depends who it is."

"What do you think though?"

"Haven't thought about it."

"You must have an opinion about it."

"Why?"

"Most people have."

"What are you fishing for?"

"I'm not fishing. I just wondered what you thought."

"I suppose it's all right for some."

"But what do you think?"

"Do you want to get engaged when you're sixteen?"

"I don't know. Depends, I suppose."

"You think we should get engaged then?"

"It's not up to me."

"You don't know what you want."

"I do. I do know. But it's no good me thinking one thing and you thinking another. It's no good me wanting to get engaged if you don't."

"I never said I didn't."

"I know you didn't."

"I bet your mother never said anything about us getting engaged."

"She did, Kenny, honest."

"Why do you want to get engaged, anyway?"

"I thought we loved each other."

"No excuse to get engaged. Folk can love each other without having to get engaged. You only need to get engaged if you're in the club. You're not in the club, are you?"

"No. Would it be different if I was?"

"How do you mean?"

"We'd have to get engaged then. Married even. We'd have no choice, would we?"

"Your mother'd have a blue fit. Her good little girl with a bun in the oven."

"Yeh," Janice says, feeling the vibration in her toes.

· · ·

That night they slept in Kenny's narrow bed in the fibreboard box behind number 472, having sneaked in as the three chimes of the Town Hall clock were echoing emptily over the flat silent roofs of the Estate. Motorway traffic hummed distantly, the faint scudding roar of lorries on the overnight run south. Their sound reminded Kenny that other places existed: that the town in which he lived had no claim on him other than that he had been born here. There was nothing to stop him and Janice packing two suitcases and catching the Yelloway coach and clearing out. They could go... almost anywhere; it was a free country.

It was warm in bed. Kenny had been feeling randy all day and couldn't get enough of her, his large heavy body almost crushing the breath from her lungs. His lack of consideration both alarmed and excited Janice: it was another of his moods she couldn't fathom, like having to deal with a stubborn and perverse animal whose brute strength carries it mindlessly forward in search of... and what that was she didn't know. She was willing to help him if only he would tell her what it was he was seeking. It annoyed her that she couldn't, even yet, understand him. After all, they were in love, so why were they not united as one person? Why did he drive himself blindly, using his strength as a battering-ram, crashing headfirst into the future as though desperate to break through a barrier that Janice couldn't see? Life was simple to her: it lay before her like a map with all the landmarks clearly shown: there was no need to fight life or to change it because what was there would, given time, fulfil all their hopes and dreams. And in any case it never did any good to fight. It never got you anywhere, and more often than not would only lead to trouble.

. . .

A week later, walking through Rochdale market with Andy some time between eight-thirty and nine o'clock in the evening, Kenny was stopped by a man in plain clothes and asked if he wouldn't mind coming along to the police station. They walked with the Detective-Constable along the Esplanade past the GPO and the

Town Hall and up the tarmacadam incline into the greyish-white block where Andy was told to wait by the desk in the sleek reception hall while Kenny was shown into a room and asked to take a seat. He smoked three cigarettes one after the other, biting his nails between drags and waiting for the Detective-Constable to reappear pushing a trolley on which a corpse lay stiff under a white sheet with a gaping bloody hole in its stomach. He knew nothing about corpses; he supposed they could be kept indefinitely in cold storage and transported all over the country in refrigerated vans. That would be their way, he felt sure; confront him with the evidence and measure the shock on his face. He stiffened his face in readiness, setting the jaw muscles in squat defiance and bringing the brows close together; he couldn't control his lips, however, except when he was dragging on the cigarette.

The Detective-Constable came in, not with a corpse on a trolley, but with a constable in uniform. They both appeared to be agreeable young men, both with sideburns, and the constable with a small black moustache. The small room seemed to Kenny to be filled with neatly-pressed suits and dark-blue uniforms and pink fleshy hands and faces. He was intimidated by their cleanliness.

"It's Kenny, isn't it?" the Detective-Constable said. He was holding two sheets of paper.

"Yeh."

"What?"

"Yeh," Kenny said, clearing his throat.

"Four-seven-two Irvine, Ashfield Valley. What's your father's name?"

"Brian."

"Brian Seddon," the Detective-Constable said, writing it down. "How old are you, Kenny?"

"Sixteen," Kenny said. "Seventeen."

The Detective-Constable waited.

"It's me birthday," Kenny blurted out. "Today."

"Many happy returns. Where do you work?"

"Haven't got a job at the moment."

"Unemployed," the Detective-Constable said, writing it down. "Have you ever been in trouble before?"

"How do you mean?"

"Have you ever been in trouble before? With the police."

Kenny swallowed. "I was picked up one time at Rochdale football ground."

"Were you charged?"

Kenny looked up at him and then down at the table. "I'm not sure. I wasn't fined or anything like that. I have to see the Juvenile Liaison Officer every month."

"Right. Yes. What about outside Rochdale? Have you ever been in trouble, you know, anywhere else?"

"No," Kenny said, almost a shade too quickly. He had nearly said Luton, almost wanted to say it. It was frightening how easy it was to give yourself away, as though something was urging you to confess everything. He lit another cigarette (his last one) and used it as camouflage to draw several deep steadying breaths. They must have got him mixed up with somebody else. They were polite enough; it was only routine; they wouldn't be so polite if it was anything serious.

The constable with the neat black moustache was looking at him quite openly. It seemed to Kenny that he almost smiled. They were friendly blokes, really, not all that much older than him. They were probably married, with children: ordinary straightforward blokes in suits and uniforms. He felt his confidence returning.

The Detective-Constable said, "What've you done with the money?"

Kenny stopped breathing. He couldn't answer the question because he hadn't the faintest idea what the Detective-Constable was on about. There hadn't been any money in the Liberal Club. Then he felt relieved; they really had confused him with somebody else. It was all right, they'd made a mistake. He felt like telling them they'd made a mistake, but instead he said:

"I haven't taken any money."

The constable opened the door, poked his head into the corridor, and closed the door again. Kenny noticed that he was practically as tall as the door.

The Detective-Constable said, "We hate fucking liars: you're a fucking liar."

"I'm not," Kenny said, "honest."

"On the 4th of January—a Friday—you did four meters on Bury Road. You broke in four flats and took seventeen quid from the meters. Right? This is a statement." He pushed a sheet of paper across the table. "Sign here," and laid a pen beside it.

"Weren't me," Kenny said. "Honest. I wasn't in Rochdale that night. I was in Heywood——"

"At the Seven Stars," the Detective-Constable said. "You got the bus to Rochdale, got the eleven o'clock bus up to Bury Road and broke in four flats and robbed the meters. Right? Anything else you want to tell us?"

"Weren't *me*."

"Keep your fucking voice down," the Detective-Constable said very quietly.

Kenny was suddenly furious. He controlled it inwardly but his stomach ached with the effort. She'd told them everything. He couldn't think. He had to tell them something quickly to make them believe he hadn't been there. He had to keep on saying he hadn't been there and eventually they would have to believe him. But why him, why had she done this to him? He couldn't credit it.

"Sign the statement," the Detective-Constable said. "Right? Don't give us any pain."

Kenny dropped his cigarette on the floor and put his heel on it.

"Pick that up," the constable said. Kenny picked it up and held it in his hand.

The Detective-Constable was looking at him across the table. The hairs in his nostrils were vibrating gently with his breathing. His shirt collar was starched and spotless, the tie in a precise triangular knot. He sighed almost imperceptibly and glanced up at the constable, muttering something that Kenny didn't catch. The constable came round the table behind the chair and leaned over him, his chin almost on Kenny's shoulder. There was a strong smell of aftershave.

"Laddie," he said, "we can't waste any more time on you. Sign the statement as you've been told. Don't be a cunt all your life."

"It weren't bloody me," Kenny protested.

"You yobboes," the constable said softly. "You are as thick as pig-shit. You are a prize cunt. I've sorted more of your lot out than you've had hot dinners. Now are you going to sign that statement—I'm asking you nicely—or do we have to make you sign it?"

Kenny stared at the piece of paper. The cigarette butt had crumbled in his fingers and bits of charred tobacco were falling to the floor. "I'm not——" he said, and the constable lost his temper and hit Kenny so hard that he fell off the chair on to his knees. The blow had been on the upper arm, right on the muscle, and his entire arm went numb. The constable kicked him on the buttocks and Kenny rolled across the floor. The two of them picked him up and Kenny was astounded at the hate in their faces. It didn't seem right to him, such hatred from these clean young men. They were married and probably had kids of their own. Surely if he asked them to be reasonable...

He found himself standing against the wall while the Detective-Constable took what seemed ages aiming a fist at his stomach; Kenny was watching his eyes as it came and he remembered that his main feeling was one of complete mystification that this young man who had walked along the Esplanade with him should be actually doing this. Kenny was angry—part of him, that is, was angry—but so frightened that the fear seemed to have drained his arms of all strength. He was afraid that if he retaliated they might do something really terrible to him. He was hit repeatedly on the arms and ribs (places where it wouldn't show) and kicked on the shins and ankles. At one point he thought he was going to cry but managed to hold it back. After five minutes or so the two young men, panting a little, sat him down on the chair and the Detective-Constable started pushing Kenny's head forward until his nose was resting on the paper.

"Today is Friday." The Detective-Constable was slightly flushed and breathing unevenly. "If you don't sign the statement now we'll keep you here over the weekend. You'll sign it Monday."

His head still bowed, Kenny said, "What will you do to me if I sign it?"

"What will we do to you if you don't sign it?"

"Can you write?" the constable said. He took hold of Kenny by the scruff of the neck and jerked him upright. "Did anything penetrate that thick skull of yours at school?" He gave a little snort of derision. "Seventeen quid. That's about your mark, you thick twat. Come on, sign."

Kenny wrote his name on the dotted line at the bottom of the paper.

He felt relieved somehow but he also felt physically sick. It wasn't that he was badly hurt—just that he wanted to go home. He couldn't think of anything better at this moment than to be sitting on the settee watching Les Dawson on the telly. He thought of Margaret sitting there in the flickering darkness and Kat eating Rice Krispies out of a bowl and his eyes filled with tears. He really thought that he was never going to see them again. That life had gone forever. His future was confined to this room and these two young men and him with a pen in his hand staring at a piece of paper with his name on it. All the alternatives had narrowed down to just this one: Kenny Seddon on his own without a friend in the world. He thought for a moment, wildly, that it was all a terrible dream; then he remembered he had no cigarettes left and knew that this time it was for real.

FAMILY TROUBLE LED
'REJECTED' YOUTH
TO THEFT — SOLICITOR

REJECTION by his father and disharmony in his family led a seventeen-year-old youth to court, a solicitor told Rochdale borough magistrates on Monday.

B—— P—— W—— of Sandridge, Ashfield Valley, admitted breaking into the Air Training Corps hut in Ashfield Valley and stealing £2.50 worth of property and cash.

W—— told police he climbed into the hut through an open window after removing wire mesh from the frame. A friend told him it was easy to get in.

Mr S. J. Greenwood, defending W——, said: "He has been rejected by his father for most of his life. His mother has left home and he doesn't know where she is. His previous court appearances, as a juvenile, were because of the disharmony which resulted in the family."

W——, said Mr Greenwood, lost a job in January, got another as a roof tiler and was then made redundant.

Police questioned W—— with a juvenile at W——'s home and were told: "We haven't done anything wrong." But a pair of drumsticks, a cap badge, a blazer badge and £1.25 were found in his possession and he admitted breaking into the hut.

W—— was sent to a detention centre. The juvenile was allowed bail and is to appear before the juvenile court on Friday.

DETENTION

GOVERNORS

G GRIFFITHS	1955–58
L F WHEELER	1958–61
W H C CARMICHAEL	1961–68
W L KILLIP BEM	1968–73
R M PARFITT	1973–

BUCKLEY HALL IS ABOUT TWO MILES TO THE NORTH OF Rochdale, just inside the borough boundary, standing in sixty-three acres of grounds with its own farm (with 50 cows), workshops, a staff of seventy including forty-nine officers in uniform, Chaplain, seamstress, part-time teachers and maintenance men, and at any one time round about 100 detainees between the ages of sixteen and twenty-one. The inner perimeter is marked by a high wire fence which encloses the main buildings and central courtyard, although access up the driveway is perfectly free and open, with beautifully tended flowerbeds and sloping lawns on either side. The Hall itself is a dignified building in grey-brown stone — what you might imagine to have been the home of a mill owner — though without the white-painted iron bars across the windows and that air of military primness which implies there is a place for everything and everything is in its place.

In a year six hundred boys (known as first custodial offenders) pass through the Detention Centre, the biggest proportion of them from Liverpool and Kirkby. Sentences are of three or six months' duration with usually one-third remission for good behaviour. The success rate, ie: those who within two years of leaving the Centre haven't got into further trouble, is estimated to be about 55 per cent. The boys are paid 20½ pence per week plus a five pence bonus; they are allowed to write (those who can write) two letters a week and one half-hour visit every fourteen days. On arrival they are classified as Grade I and kept under close supervision for two weeks; after two weeks a report is compiled on each boy and subject to him having made satisfactory progress he is allowed to complete Grade I and then re-classified as Grade II, which means he can work outside the perimeter fence.

Kenny came in with three other lads, two from the 'Pool and one from Blackburn. In the van he found out that between them they had two cases of burglary, one of taking and driving without consent, and one of common assault. They were issued with shirts, underclothes, overalls and boots, each given a number to memorise, and spent the rest of the day seeing in turn the Doctor, Warden, Education Officer, Welfare Officer and House Officer.

Standing in line with the other three newcomers dressed in strange, baggy clothes he was given a summary of the day's routine by an officer in a peaked cap with the chain of a whistle looped from his breast pocket:

"You rise at six-thirty. Wash, shave if you have to, and prepare for breakfast at ten minutes past seven. Parade at eight o'clock. Your duties will be assigned to you for the day. Work during the morning. Parade at twelve o'clock. Lunch from twelve-thirty to one-thirty. Parade at one-thirty. Back to your assigned duties for the afternoon — by the way, one hour's PE during either the morn-ing or afternoon. Parade at five o'clock. Wash and change for tea. Tea from five-thirty till six-fifteen. Evening classes commence at six-fifteen till eight o'clock: from eight o'clock to nine-fifteen, recreation: darts, cards, chess, etcetera, TV at the weekend. The library is open if you wish to use it. Supper at nine-fifteen, then wash, undress, bed and lights out at nine forty-five sharp.

"Now, rules and regulations: there are ten work periods during the five-day week and from one to three points awarded each day for conduct and general behaviour. You will note that smoking is not allowed at any time. You will address all officers, teachers and other members of staff as 'Sir', rise and stand to attention when-ever they enter the room and remain at attention until instructed otherwise. Disciplinary matters will be referred to your House Officer, the Assistant Warden and the Warden, in that order and depending on the nature of the offence. Is that clear? Any ques-tions? Fall out."

Kenny had always thought he was tough until he came up against the Scousers in Buckley Hall: they frightened the living daylights out of him. He learnt his lesson that first day when a scuf-fle broke out in the corridor and, standing innocently by, he was butted in the face and had his nose burst. Two officers appeared and sorted it out before it could develop into anything serious, but a nod to Kenny was as good as a wink: steer clear of the Scousers and never, under any circumstances, pick a fight with any of them. They were a breed he hadn't encountered in large numbers before — not just hard on the surface but hard all the way through, tough as old boots — and with such a strong accent that the language they spoke was almost incomprehensible to anyone else.

His first meal in the dining-hall at teatime surprised him: it was good nosh and plenty of it. He was nervous, which made him hun-gry, and he wiped every trace of baked beans from his plate with a slice of dry bread and washed it down with strong tea. He felt a lot better with his stomach full and began to take an interest in this strange new environment of rows of lads all dressed alike and officers in dark uniforms standing at either end of the hall and— something he hadn't expected—an air about the place of comrade-ship, almost a cosy family atmosphere with the lads bent over their plates and now and then a smothered snigger of laughter or a brief snatch of conversation. It seemed as though talking wasn't allowed at mealtimes, though the officers (did they call them screws?) didn't appear to enforce the rule with absolute strictness.

One of the Liverpool lads nudged Kenny and said in a murmur, "There's a bloke over there looking at you," and when Kenny glanced up saw Skush at a table near the window raising and low-ering his eyebrows. He looked fatter and there was colour in his cheeks; neither were his eyes the same staring watery brown.

The first night was the worst. Kenny and the other three were each locked in a tiny cubicle with a bed and a wooden chair. It was explained to them that tomorrow they would be given a bed in one of the dormitories but tonight they had to sleep alone. At eight o'clock the doors were locked and the light switched off and from the window all that could be seen were dark, unfamiliar shapes on a background of blackest night. Kenny lay in the darkness, the stiff laundered sheets against his skin, his feet confined by the regulation folded bedclothes; it was very quiet, no motorway traffic, no chim-ing Town Hall clock, none of that grating metallic sound of garage doors sliding shut. He had been brave all day, preoccupied with the newness and strangeness of everything, but now his bravery had ebbed away and he began to feel very small inside, like a child almost. He wasn't going to cry, he would resist crying with all his might. He was a grown-up lad in a Detention Centre; one amongst a hundred other grown-up lads; locks and doors and fences sepa-rated them from the outside world. In fact he could hardly believe that the real outside world still existed. Were there people in pubs at this moment? Were Andy, Fester, Crabby and the rest of them pinting it somewhere right now? It seemed as though the rest of the world had stopped dead, vanished, ceased to exist, and he, Kenny, was alone in the darkness with the sound of his own heartbeats and the scrape of the sheets on his skin. He wasn't going to cry, though, he would make sure of that.

He tried not to think of Janice. But in trying not to think about her she had entered his mind and he couldn't stop himself thinking about her. He would have been strong inside — stronger, any-way — if he could be assured that she still loved him. Vera had been to blame for telling the police, she had given evidence against him, but because he hadn't been allowed to see Janice (or she hadn't been allowed to see him) it wasn't clear in his mind whether she was equally to blame or had been forced to tell on him. She must have been forced, she must have been ... she must still love him ... there was nothing else he could think. Her mother had wormed the truth out of her, that's how it must have happened. Vera — Christ, that woman! — the hate in her, the nastiness, the spite! What had he done to deserve such hatred? It took his breath away even now, here, away from everything, to recall that look on her face.

Margaret had stood by him: thank God for her and bless her, the old lady had stuck up for him. She had been near crying herself, but she had kept it bottled up inside. He had actually felt proud of her, they had hugged each other, and he'd felt all the suppressed move-ments in her chest battering against him. It showed at times like these who really cared and who didn't. She was still his mother and he was still her son: they were a family and there would always be some love for him there. He pictured her at home with Kat, not many miles away on the other side of town, the two of them watch-ing TV. He conjured up the warm peaceful flat in his mind, the stairs leading down to the passage, his door on the left and behind it his room and inside it his bed, empty now of course and unslept in: a huge sob came up from the depths of his stomach and he had to let it all out.

. . .

Four meals a day: Kenny hadn't eaten so well in a long time. He was put in the same dormitory as Skush, who had done a month and, subject to a satisfactory report, was about to move from Grade I to Grade II.

"Have you put on weight since you've been here?" Kenny asked.

"Yeh, you either put it on or take it off. The screws have a joke. They say if the police caught you before you came in they won't catch you after you get out."

"What have you got left to do?"

"Another month if I get full remission. You'll have two months to do if you keep your nose clean." He used the jargon unselfconsciously. Kenny had always liked Skush but never admired him before; but this was an old lag speaking.

He said, "Does anyone ever try to make a break for it?"

"A few do. A few Scousers, but it's pointless because if you get caught you lose your remission. Watch out for the psychos."

"Who are them?" Kenny said, worrying his thumbnail.

"Some of the blokes in here are real nutters." He screwed his finger into his head. "They should be locked away. If they catch you looking at them they go for you. One of the lads nearly got knifed last week."

"Knifed?" Kenny said. The word made him shiver and brought cold sweat to his forehead. But in a peculiar way he felt safer in here than he had outside: they couldn't pick him up for that now, he was off the streets, out of the reckoning.

"What are the screws like?"

Skush shrugged. "Not bad. Play fair with them and they play fair with you. It's not them you have to bother about, it's some of the head cases they've stuck in here because they don't know where else to put them."

Kenny was about to ask for a few names to avoid when an officer came in and they both stood to attention.

"What you lot doing?"

"Come to fetch my gym-kit, sir," Skush said.

"Who are you?"

"Seddon."

"Sir."

"Seddon, sir."

"Number?"

"437..." Kenny's face was convulsed. "437 ... 972."

"What are you doing here?"

"Mopping the floor. Sir."

"Don't take all day. Carry on."

.   .   .

In the evenings after tea there were classes in a dozen subjects, including English for those who literacy age was under seven; over the two months they were inside it was hoped to raise their standard to twelve plus. Kenny scraped through the compulsory English test and was able to choose the subjects he wanted. He decided on Art, Woodwork and Interior Decoration. Each lecture was complete in itself because with a class which gained a few and lost a few every week it was impossible to maintain any continuity. The teachers were part-time, from nearby schools, or local tradesmen who came in two or three evenings a week.

The days seemed interminably long at first and the nights were even worse: but after a week, what with the never-ending round of cleaning duties, PE, parades, meals, evening classes and an hour spent playing cards or, at the weekend, watching television, the hours lost their dragging inertia and merged into a passing blur and before you knew it it was time for bed, lights out, and a sound heavy sleep induced by a day spent in the fresh air and continual activity. For when you weren't working you were exercising, and when not exercising, eating, and when not eating, studying, and when not studying, sleeping ...

Still the worse time, though, was before sleep came, lying in the silent breathing dormitory with the occasional rustle of sheets as someone relieved his sexual urge and invariably the voice of a Scouser trying by turns to antagonise the other lads or make them laugh. One of the lads in Kenny's dormitory who everyone treated as a simpleton—an enormous bloke with broad shoulders who went by the name of Desperate Dan—always waited till lights out and would then say in a loud Scouse voice:

"Who'd like to look at my big toe?"

This set off a chain-reaction of wisecracks which mainly had to do with bum boys, giant pricks and kissing the Pope's ring. Skush had warned Kenny to be on the look-out for queers but so far he hadn't been approached or noticed anything suspicious going on. He couldn't believe that Desperate Dan was a pouf, though the thought that he might be scared him to death.

He had never written a letter in his life—except for forging sick-notes at school—so he didn't bother writing to Margaret; he thought once of writing to Janice but couldn't think what to say, or rather what he wanted to say couldn't be put in a letter. He would wait for Margaret's first visit and ask her to pass a message to Jan, or better still get Jan to visit him, which is what he wanted most of all. He still wouldn't accept that she had deserted him: it was Vera, it had to be, who had turned her daughter against him. He wasn't resentful or even mildly annoyed that Jan had got off with a warning. The police hadn't been too hard on her, probably because she didn't have a record: the general consensus had been that Kenny had corrupted her and led her astray. That was how things worked in the world and Kenny was the last one to be dismayed or even surprised.

His report after two weeks was favourable, which meant that in another two weeks, all being well, he would be Grade II. The days settled down into a set routine, eating, working, studying, sleeping, and for this reason anything out of the ordinary was even more noticeable — such as the time when the bloke with four kids went berserk.

It happened in the recreation room one evening when everyone was peaceably reading, playing cards or just talking. As might be expected he was a Scouser, a thin nervous lad with a prominent Adam's apple and tattoos on his skinny arms. Without warning and for no apparent reason he ran into the wall and started screaming. A couple of the lads tried to restrain him but he was demented and wouldn't be held; he shook them off, pushed his fist through the window and turned his wrist against the jagged glass. The walls were sprayed with blood and a pack of cards on a nearby table was ruined; spots of blood were later found on the television screen in the far corner of the room. Kenny stood and watched as two officers picked him up off the floor and, without waiting for a stretcher, ran with him to the hospital ward.

"Psycho," somebody said.

"What's up with him?" Kenny asked.

"He's married with four kids. His wife's been doing a bit on the side and he wants to get released quick and sort her out."

"It hits married fellas the hardest," Desperate Dan said. "That's why you want to steer clear of women," leering vacantly in Kenny's direction.

"Will he get out?"

"He'll be shoved in hospital," somebody said, "and then he'll be back. They're not that stupid."

"What about his wife?"

"What about her?"

It costs between £25 – £30 a week to keep a boy in a Detention Centre, though the cost would be very much greater if the place wasn't to some extent self-sufficient: cleaning, maintenance and general repairs are done by the boys themselves with guidance from trades officers and workmen. The workshops, where Grade II detainees spend one month, produce concrete kerb and paving stones which are sent to other Borstals and Detention Centres to make roadworks and repair existing ones — which is why such establishments are always well looked after, neat and shipshape to the point of obsessiveness. Another workshop makes moulded rubber wheels under contract to a manufacturer of hand-trucks and trolleys. The farm supplies milk, cheese and eggs to the kitchens and any surplus is taken by local farmers. After two months the boys on six-month sentences are allowed outside in small working parties, either to the farm or helping Rochdale Corporation Works Department maintain roadworks in the district.

Behind the main building is the sports field, surrounded by a wire-mesh fence with barbed-wire along the top, and the Centre has a football team in a northern amateur league; all games are played at home. On Sundays the Chaplain (C of E) holds a service, and there is a mass for Catholics, which those who profess to be atheists can opt out of but which most of the detainees, who've never been near a church since their twelfth birthdays, if at all, attend without objection.

Kenny gradually found his feet in Buckley Hall and after the trauma of Margaret's first visit it slowly began to dawn on him that compared with some of the other lads (excluding the illiterates) he didn't have much of a clue: he had always reckoned himself to be

pretty smart but there were some blokes—one in particular—
who had really got it all weighed up. Over a game of cards in the
recreation room Kenny happened to mention that he had worked
at Haigh's and Woolworth's and a few other places; Barry Keesig
pulled a sour expression and called him a pillock to his face. Work
was out, a mug's game.

"What did you get at Haigh's?" Barry Keesig asked, dealing a
hand of crib.

"Just over eleven," Kenny said.

"Clear?"

"No, nine pounds-summat clear."

"Nine quid for a week's work." Barry Keesig smiled in his
snarling way and shook his head. He had a long flat contemptuous
face with a rectangular jaw and eyes like slits. He was the kind of
bloke whose opinion everyone respects, though he never went out
of his way to gain that respect and didn't seem bothered one way or
another. "I could make double that in an afternoon."

"Doing what?"

"Using this"—tapping his head.

"Yeh but doing what though?"

"Not robbing fucking meters for a start," somebody said.

"Who asked you?" Kenny said, suddenly angry. He was willing
to learn but he wasn't prepared to let any of them put him down.
They had all been caught, hadn't they, no matter how clever they
might have been?

"Most of them in here are bums," Barry Keesig said.
"Deadbeats. If you're going to make it pay you've got to get organ-
ised. And it's no good going for a few measly quid—it's got to be
real money."

"The cars is a good number," somebody said.

"For that you've got to have the gear. Workshop. Spraying
equipment. Log books. Number plates. And it means driving them

down south somewhere. Hard cash, that's the only way, no frigging about. Straight in, lift it, and out again."

"Post offices," Kenny said, coming up with a positive thought.

"Yeh," Barry Keesig said. "Or better still, factories. There's always loads of cash in factories. Three or four of you, say, in overalls; get in at dinner time with the rest of them and have a shuftie round. Wages office. Canteen. Cloakrooms. Christ, you can't go wrong."

Kenny's hands trembled a little as he held the cards. Barry was right, it was dead easy. An afternoon's work and you could get away with, what — forty or fifty dabs each — enough to last a fortnight. He felt himself getting excited at the idea.

The following day he received a letter from Margaret saying that she hadn't yet been able to get in touch with Janice. Kenny had asked her to persuade Janice to visit him but he knew that if Mrs Singleton got to hear of it she wouldn't allow it. The problem was how to get to Jan without Vera finding out. He put the letter in his locker.

Skush said, "Cheer up, it may never happen."

"It's all right for you, you're getting out on Friday. Lucky twat."

"It comes to us all," Skush said.

"Hey," Kenny said, thinking.

"What?"

"If you happen to see Jan when you get out tell her to come and see me. Will you?"

"Yeh," Skush said. "If I see her knocking around."

"What are you going to do when you leave?"

"Get a job, I suppose. I'll have to; the old fella will be on at me."

"Have you got rid of the habit?"

"I have now. Give me two weeks outside and I'll probably be on heroin."

"It's a fucking hard life," Kenny said.

"If you don't weaken."

Kenny became good friends with Barry Keesig and they talked a lot about what they were going to do when they left Buckley Hall. Barry Keesig had three months to serve — two months longer than Kenny — but they promised to keep in touch and meet up when they were both outside. Kenny had forgotten, or so it seemed to him, what it was like to be a free agent. He watched Skush walking down the stairs with a brown paper parcel under his arm and it was as though this life, inside HM Borstal and Detention Centre, behind the high wire fence, was the only one he had ever known. Skush was walking off the edge of the planet, away from the real world and into the mysterious Outside. Of course he, Kenny, could remember what it had been like before, but in an odd way it seemed unreal, a distant dream filled with people who were like actors in a film he had seen a long time ago and only faintly remembered. The place inside — Inside — had a life of its own; even the sky looked different, and for the first time in his life Kenny noticed such things as trees and grass and even heard the birds singing. He came to know the buildings, the courtyards, the workshops, the sports field in such intimate detail that he found it hard to recall his own bedroom at 472, Ashfield Valley: this was reality, here and now, the other was a memory from a half-forgotten past life.

Sometimes he was shaken out of his dream-state as when, for instance, three Scousers went for him in the showers and nearly broke his wrist. There was no motive for their action — none that Kenny could fathom, anyway — unless it was simply that they had stared at him and he had stared back. They waited, with cunning calculation, until the others were clear of the shower, and then closed in with fists and heels, Kenny slipping on the wet tiles and attempting to save himself by the reflex action of his left arm. The next thing he knew it was as if someone had inserted a white-hot needle between his hand and the protruding ulna on the point of his wrist, and he nearly fainted with the pain. Two of them held his arms flat against the streaming tiles while the other stood astride him and worked his heavy hanging cock into life, arriving quickly at a climax and masturbating into Kenny's face. The spray of water soon washed the sperm away but he didn't forget their faces in a hurry.

VISITORS

THE ROOM CONTAINED PERHAPS A DOZEN SMALL TABLES, AT each table two straight-backed wooden chairs set facing each other. The boys were in their places and most of the other visitors had arrived and sat down when Margaret appeared and came through the tables to where Kenny was intent on the index fingernail of his right hand. It was bitten almost to the half-moon.

"Well," Margaret said, smiling in the way she had rehearsed. "You're looking all right, love"—spending longer than was necessary in sitting down, straightening her chair, brushing invisible specks off her coat while she thought what to say next—"how are they treating you?"

Kenny stared at her.

"I've brought you some chocolate," Margaret said as if suddenly remembering, and she put two half-pound bars on the table. "You're not allowed cigarettes, are you? I bet it's made you stop, has it? One good thing, I suppose. Kat sends her love."

Kenny said, "Why have you not said owt?"

"What?"

"Why've you not said owt about Janice?"

"Give me time, love, I've only just got here; I told you in the letter I hadn't had chance to see her. She's——"

"You said you'd get her to come and see me. Why didn't she come with you?" Kenny wasn't aware that he was speaking louder, though people at the other tables had paused a moment to listen.

"I'll tell you if you'll give me time," his mother said in a rushed whisper. "I tried to get in touch with her——"

"You told me that in the letter," Kenny said stolidly.

"*Lis*ten." She cleared her throat and went on hurriedly in a low voice. "I had to be careful, didn't I? You know very well what

Mrs Singleton would have said. I just couldn't go up there or send a letter, could I? Anyway——"

Kenny waited. "Anyway what?" he said.

"Well," Margaret said, fidgeting. "Janice couldn't have come up."

"Why not?"

"She's gone away. Her mother's sent her away."

"Where to?"

"Halifax."

"*Halifax?*" Kenny said, his swollen eyes staring out of his head. "What the fuck's she doing in Halifax?"

"All I know is she's gone to stay with relatives," Margaret said, trying to keep from meeting the eyes of the other visitors.

It took Kenny a moment to assimilate this information and a further moment to realise its implications. He said slowly and with real hatred, "The cow. She's done it on purpose to stop Jan coming to see me." He knew why. He shouldn't have plonked it. That was his big mistake. The cow was jealous. She couldn't stand the thought of him and Janice wanting to see each other, to be together. His first reaction was to hit back in some way, tell somebody what he had done, make the cow suffer. But that wouldn't do any good, and if Jan were to find out…He ripped the wrapping paper off the chocolate and broke off a huge piece in his mouth. A trickle of dark-brown saliva ran down his chin.

"What's wrong with your wrist?" Margaret asked.

"I fell on it."

"You ought to save that chocolate."

"What for, Christmas?" Kenny said savagely.

"Never mind, love, only another four weeks and then——"

"And then I'll sort *her* out."

"Now don't say that—you mustn't talk that way." Margaret suddenly felt it necessary to become firm. "It's all through her and her mother that you're where you are now. You'll stay away, do you hear? We had enough of Vera Singleton in the court. It's through them you got into trouble in the first place."

Kenny gazed at her uncomprehendingly. "How do you work that out?"

"Breaking into the flats," Margaret said, as if explaining an obvious fact to a recalcitrant child. "If you'd never met Janice in the first place you'd never have thought of taking that money. She probably put the idea into your head. She was always quiet, that girl, I grant you, but nobody's that quiet; there's usually a bit of wickedness lurking somewhere. You haven't always been an angel but you never got into any real trouble till you started associating with her."

Kenny's chest moved with suppressed feeling but he breathed out slowly and the emotion subsided.

"Well," Margaret said, "did you?"

"No," Kenny said.

"There you are then," she said for want of something better to say. She seemed at a loss for words. And then, abruptly, "I'd better tell you. You'll find out sooner or later. Janice is pregnant."

Kenny bit off a hunk of chocolate. "Oh aye," he said.

"More reason to stay away."

"You reckon," Kenny said.

"We've enough on our plate without a bastard in the family. This year hasn't started well for us but let's not make it any worse." She put her hand on his, the one that held the half-eaten bar of chocolate. "Love, you'll be out in four weeks. Your dad and me will help you. Forget her, all right?" He didn't respond. She tried to smile. "All right?"

Kenny didn't take his eyes off her as he crammed the rest of the chocolate into his mouth.

. . .

[203]

The boys filed past the officer on duty at the door of the dining-hall, collected their food at the serving-hatch and took their places; the officer scrutinised each boy as he went past, looked for a moment into their indifferent eyes as if to remind them of their position and keep them in check for a further few hours. Not that there was any danger of them rebelling: it was merely standard procedure based on official policy and institutional psychology.

Kenny sat with Barry Keesig and one or two other lads who formed their group, wolfing his food, as far removed from his surroundings as it was possible to be. He was counting the days. He was being very careful to keep his nose clean. He was also plotting revenge. He had, so to speak, clamped his mind shut so that nothing existed beyond certain set priorities: count the days, keep out of trouble, think and plan and scheme for the day of reckoning. There was Janice and Vera to sort out; that was Priority One. There was the future with Barry and the other lads to think about; that was Priority Two. And he hadn't forgotten about the three boys in the showers; that was another sort of Priority altogether, yes definitely another sort.

There was a commotion at the end of the table — nothing serious, just a few of them flicking spoonfuls of rice pudding at one another — and the officer walked along the line watching the faces for a clue as to what was going on, who was causing it, and why. Everyone was eating studiously, hiding their smirks behind spoons and dishes. As the officer turned back to his post a sticky gob of rice pudding landed on Kenny's forehead and bits of it splattered in his eye. He wiped the mess away and swore under his breath.

"No talking," said the officer coming up behind and pushed his face into the dish. There were snorts and muffled laughter along the table; Kenny again wiped his face and sat without moving; he refused to meet anyone's eye because he suspected that if he did there would be no telling what might happen. He had his Three

Priorities to think of and could allow nothing to get in the way of them. Count the days: keep your nose clean: plot and plan for sweet revenge.

Andy came to see him on the next visitors' day and it seemed to Kenny that, with two weeks to go, he could scent freedom. His guts ached with the desire to get out, to be Outside. Life somehow seemed to be waiting for him now — as though suddenly he had been given a purpose and had something to accomplish.

"You look thinner," Andy said.

"Yeh, the screws have a joke about it," Kenny said. "They say if the cops caught before you came in they won't catch you after you get out."

"Not long to go now."

"Thirteen days."

"Is that all?"

"If I keep my nose clean and get full remission."

"What are you going to do when you get out?"

"I got a few plans," Kenny said, his eyes veiled and heavy-lidded. "Met some blokes in here I'm going to team up with."

"Doing what?"

"Oh, different things."

Andy went away, suitably impressed, Kenny felt. Of course they were in different leagues now. The old days had gone forever. No more of that childish pissing about selling blues and bombers at the Pendulum or taking a Paki for two or three dabs. He wouldn't waste his sweat on that now. And to think he'd been nabbed for just seventeen quid! He must have been simple.

Each day appeared to stretch out longer than the last so that it seemed he would never reach the end. Spring was coming too, and Kenny felt a strong physical urge to break free of this set, orderly, regulation existence. At times he was almost exploding with suppressed action, like an engine at full power chained to the track. He began to sleep badly and went on sick-parade to ask for some tablets. The doctor gave him three which Kenny was on the point of taking and then decided to save. For twelve days he saved three a day, hiding them in a matchbox underneath his locker. He hadn't clearly decided what he was going to do with them; it was instinct that told him they might come in useful.

Three days before he was due to be released, Kenny received a letter from Margaret saying that she had seen Janice and her mother shopping in Yorkshire Street. Janice was looking well, Margaret said, although she hadn't spoken to her.

"Don't do anything stupid when you get out," Barry Keesig told him.

"Such as?"

"No bird's worth it. You'll be on a loser if you start something: they keep an eye on you for at least a year after."

"They'll have to sweat dustbin lids to pin anything on me," Kenny said.

"Just watch it, Seddon, that's all."

"Okay Keesig."

Kenny walked out of Buckley Hall on a bright, cold March morning, a brown paper parcel under his arm and enough bus fare in his pocket to get home. The sky was a fresh, washed blue; it looked a lot different on the Outside. He had counted the days, kept his nose clean, had his revenge. In exchange for a small favour Desperate Dan had collared the boy who had masturbated in Kenny's face and between the two of them they had forced all thirty-six tablets down his throat. Kenny was there to see the boy lose consciousness but didn't stay around to discover what else Desperate Dan had in mind.

END

IT IS VERA, NOT JANICE AT THE DOOR AS HE HAD HOPED, and Kenny barges past her and is halfway up the stairs before she can find her voice. The TV is blaring out to an empty living-room and Kenny stands in the middle of the floor breathing hard, his fists working. The fact that Janice isn't here disconcerts him. He had thought up a plan in his mind. Now he doesn't know what to do next — except maybe put his boot through the television screen and kick the furniture to pieces.

Vera says, "Outside. Come on, you bloody bastard. You can see she isn't here."

"Where is she?" Kenny says without turning round.

"She's not here, I've told you. If you don't leave I'm calling the police. I mean it."

"I said where the fuck is she?" Kenny says, staring straight ahead at the wall above the television screen.

"Don't threaten me," Vera says. "Don't swear at me. If you're not out of this flat in one minute I'm calling the police. Don't think I won't do, because I will. We've had enough of you. Janice as well, your fighting and troublemaking and getting into bother. You're out now but they'll put you back in bloody fast if I tell them you've been round here pestering us."

"Look," Kenny says, turning round to face her. She sees that his eyes are bulging and bloodshot, and the finger he points at her is shaking. "I don't want any more out of you, you old cow. It was you landed me in it. I want to see Janice, it's got nothing to do with you, so you'd better tell me where she is."

"Oh aye?" Vera says, stepping inside the room. "Or what will you do? You're a mug, Kenny, do you know that? Straight out of borstal and straightaway you come round here making threats. One word from me, the police would be here in ten minutes and you wouldn't have a leg to stand on." Her voice suddenly rises and she puts her hands on her hips. "Now are you going to clear out this minute or do I have to bloody call them?"

"Do what you like," Kenny says. "I want to see Janice first. You sent her away to keep her from seeing me, didn't you? Fucking interfering jealous old cow, that's all you are."

"Jealous of what?" Vera says. "Jealous of you? Jealous of *you*? My God, I'd be jealous of Quasimodo if I was jealous of you."

"You sent her away to Halifax."

"You heard about that, did you?" Vera says, her head nodding mechanically. "Well it had nowt to do with keeping her away from you. She wouldn't have been up to see you even if she hadn't gone away. It was to clear up your bloody handiwork, you big dozy lummox. Had your fun and left our Janice to cope on her own with what came after. That's bloody typical of you, a selfish ignorant pig like you."

"Where is she?"

"If you think I'd tell you——"

"Where is she?" Kenny says again. "I know she's not still in Halifax because she's been seen in Rochdale …" There is a thought niggling him but as yet he can't place it. He rushes on headlong: "You can't keep us away from each other. I know she wants to see me——"

"That's where you're wrong," Vera says tartly. She strides across the room to turn the television off. "She doesn't. That's where you're bloody wrong. Do you really think after what you did that she wants to see you again? You must want your bloody slates attending to. You!" She screws up her face as though at an unpleasant smell. "Somebody who's been in borstal! Who can't hold a job down! Who gets a girl into trouble and leaves her to fend for herself!"

"Look, woman," Kenny says quietly but getting really angry. "I didn't know anything about that till I was inside, did I? Did I? What did you expect me to do—break out of the place? And by that time she was in Halifax anyway..." The same thought continues to niggle him. He stares at Vera, his eyes protruding under the heavy lids, and says slowly, "You sent her away to get rid of it." He is genuinely shocked by this. He wanders round the room looking at the furniture.

Standing by the television set Vera says, "What did you expect? Did you think I'd let her have it? Your bastard? You must be bloody thicker than I thought you were. Do you think I'd allow my daughter to be lumbered with a kid of yours?" The venom is spilling out now. "A girl that age having to bring up a child whose father isn't man enough to hold down a job for two minutes. You must be bloody joking. I wouldn't give a brat of yours house-room. What, lumbering my Janice with a kid and her still at school? *Your* kid? Jesus Christ!"

Kenny comes partly to his senses and stops looking at the furniture to gaze at Vera. She holds her ground but for the first time begins to realise the strength within him and the dangerous nature of the situation. She has to get rid of him, she can't keep him talking, not with Janice in the bedroom.

"You fucking twat," Kenny says. "You made her have an abortion. You forced her into it. What's up with you, are you mad or something?"

"Oh," Vera says. "Oh yes. You'd have kept it, would you? You'd have supported it, would you, on bloody nothing, on sweet F.A. I can just see it—aye—a dead-leg like you, settling down with a wife and kiddie. You can't support yourself without robbing folk. The way I treated you, as one of the family, eating here, sleeping here, and all you can do is steal money from me. That's all the thanks I get. I might have known it, a bloody deadbeat like you."

"Aye," says Kenny cunningly, "one of the family all right. You weren't so bloody choosy when I slept here, were you? Couldn't keep your hands off me dick——"

"Shut *up*," Vera says. "Shut your fucking dirty mouth. And get out. Get out, I'm calling the police. I mean it this time."

"Jealousy, that's all it is. I knew it."

"I will," Vera says. "I will call them," going for the telephone. Kenny moves forward, not standing in her way, but adopting an attitude which makes her think twice. She stands with her white strained face, arm reaching out, uncertain what to do.

"Go on," Kenny says. "Fucking call them. Go on." He would really like her to do it because it is the excuse he needs. Their mutual hatred feeds on itself: the absolute repulsion of two people who have once liked each other. Strangers could not have loathed each other with half the intensity.

"I will," Vera says.

"Go on then."

"Don't kid yourself I won't do it."

"I know you will," Kenny says. "I wouldn't expect anything else of a slag like you. That's why I feel sorry for Jan, being brought up by somebody who trades it all over Rochdale. What do you charge, Vera, five quid a night and ten bob for a quick knee-trembler? Christ, it's a wonder they don't need climbing boots and a rope-ladder when they have a go at you. Course they can always get help from the blokes already in there. Stand on each others' shoulders and form a rescue party."

"Right," Vera says. "Out of my way." She swings at him and Kenny parries it easily. He raises his fist as if to strike her. "You just bloody do," Vera says. "I can have you right now for breach of the peace. You lay a finger on me and it'll be assault as well."

"Yeh?" Kenny says. "You'd better make sure you're in a fit state to call the police."

"What?" Vera says. "What? You threatening me? Are you bloody stupid or something? You've only just been let out and you're asking to be shoved right back inside — only this time it won't be just borstal."

"That won't help you though, will it?" Kenny says.

"Don't talk so bloody daft," Vera says.

"No——" Kenny says, and stops. He has noticed a cardigan on the arm of a chair. It is Janice's cardigan. He looks swiftly round the room, realising how stupid he has been, and sees two half-empty beakers of tea on the coffee table. "She's here," he says, going out quickly before Vera can get in his way, along the passage to the door of Janice's bedroom and grasping the handle. It is locked. Vera comes up behind him. "Don't open the door," she calls out in a voice thin with panic. "Come on, you bloody bastard," getting hold of his arm and trying to drag him away.

"Jan?" Kenny says.

"Don't open the door," Vera says, striking him on the shoulder.

"Jan, it's me," Kenny says. He hunches his body to protect himself from Vera's attack, then, losing his temper, suddenly snarls and lashes out backwards with his fist. Vera is thrown against the wall.

"I'll get the police, Janice, I'll get the police. Don't open the door."

"Jan, open the door," Kenny says, "it's me, Kenny."

"Janice!" Vera screams.

"Fuck *off*," Kenny yells, swinging at her again and missing. She tries to kick him but Kenny thumps her in the chest and she falls on the floor.

"He's attacking me, he's insane," Vera screams. "Don't open the door whatever you do." She gets to her feet and runs into the living-room.

"Are you coming with me, Jan?" Kenny says. "Don't be scared, she won't hurt you. Are you all right? I know about the kid, I know she made you get rid of it. It doesn't matter, honestly. We can still go away, the two of us. Don't be frightened of your mother, she won't hurt you. Janice? *Janice?*" He bangs on the door with his fist. He can break the door down easily, he knows that, he can handle that without any trouble. What he can't understand is why she won't answer him. Why won't she talk to him? He feels strangely weak because of this. The least she can do is talk to him after all he's been through. He can hear Vera speaking in the living-room. He bangs on the door again, becoming desperate. This is the one thing he has; the rest doesn't matter if he has this. She can't let him down, she can't do, it isn't fair. He's done his share, he's waited two months, he's counted the days.

"Janice," Kenny yells. "Open this fucking door!"

There is a sound he can't identify — yet something human — behind the door. He grasps the handle but doesn't attempt to force it.

"Jan," Kenny says in a quiet, reasonable voice, "please open the door. I only want to talk to you. Look, if you don't want to come away with me it's all right. I'm not going to force you or anything. Let me just talk to you at least. Your mother won't touch you, honestly, I promise." He waits for a moment. There is another sound behind the door, as though somebody is standing very close to it, leaning on it, yet almost not daring to breathe. Kenny puts his mouth to the door; there can be no more than an inch or so separating them.

"Jan?" he says softly. He can hear breathing.

"Go away," Janice says.

In the living-room Vera has put the phone down and is lighting a cigarette to steady her nerves. She takes a long deep drag and looks at her watch.

"Jan," Kenny says. "For fuck's sake."

"They'll be here any minute," Vera calls out. "Then we'll see how tough you are. Striking a woman, that's just about your bloody mark."

Kenny slams the door once with his fist and runs out of the flat and down the stairs. It is now completely dark and the yellow street-lights are shining palely as the cold northern night comes on; it isn't raining but there is the threat of it in the air. He looks towards town and then walks along Bury Road in the opposite direction.

BOROUGH MAGISTRATES

WEDNESDAY

PROBATION OFFENCE — K—— H——, aged nineteen, of no fixed address, was, sent to Manchester Crown Court to be dealt with for a breach of probation. The order had been made by the court in March 1973 when H—— was convicted of burglary and theft. He was ordered to report to Rochdale probation officer, Mrs Jean Greenhalgh. But Mrs Greenhalgh told magistrates H—— had failed to report to her from last May. He had given himself up to the police at Kidderminster, she added.

AFTERWORD

USUALLY I HAVE ONLY THE HAZIEST NOTION OF HOW A particular novel came to be written — the spark that ignited the idea in the first place. This one is the exception; I know exactly when and where and even why *Rule of Night* came into being.

It was one Saturday afternoon in the early Seventies. I was standing on the terraces at Spotland, a keen Rochdale supporter (someone has to be; we each have our cross to bear), though from a distance of 30 years I can't remember who we were playing that day. In the novel I reprinted an item from the *Rochdale Observer*, 'Soccer Mob Runs Wild', about a match against Blackurn Rovers (imagine — the Dale playing Blackburn Rovers!) when 'a mob of about 100 Rovers supporters', according to the report, ran amok through the town centre, breaking windows and creating other kinds of mayhem. Although I'm pretty sure this wasn't the afternoon or the match in question, no doubt I drew on it as useful fodder and background for my book. This was the era of the 'bovver' boy, usually a skinhead: a new breed of identifiable hooligan with his cropped hair/shaven skull, braces on display as a fashion accessory, jeans cut off below the knee and bulging, menacing Doc Marten bovver-boots. You could spot his type coming a mile off — thank goodness — which gave you time to cross the road out of harm's way.

They were starting to be a nuisance at football matches, even at Rochdale with crowds of less than 2,000. Now and then you'd see a flurry of activity on the terraces, some pushing and shoving, and a fight would break out. (I'm almost certain this was before the fans were segregated but wouldn't swear to it.) Anyway, on this particular afternoon the police waded in behind the goals, grabbed this

Dale yobbo and frog-marched him past the Main Stand and up the players' tunnel to the jeers, obscene catcalls and flying spittle of the home fans. I can see the lad now, arm locked up his back, bent over nearly double by the copper, glaring at the crowd with a kind of sullen bravado. Not a pretty sight. And the thought went through my mind: the crowd have worked themselves up into such a blind fury that they don't see a human being any more; what they see is an animal, one that deserves all it gets; yet this lad has a mum and dad, and mates, maybe a job, possibly a girlfriend — in other words he was no different in all essentials from the folk jeering and spitting at him.

To be honest I didn't feel much sympathy for him personally, and I had little doubt he was a nasty piece of work. But still I was curious. Mainly because I hadn't a clue what went on inside that shaven skull, what he thought about, how he saw the world. In other words, what made him tick. So the desire to find the answers (or some answers at least) to these questions fired my imagination — and being a writer of fiction and not a journalist, I decided to tackle the subject by dreaming up a story and creating characters based on people I talked to and the experiences they told me about. Maybe that way I would gain some understanding of the (to me) biggest mystery of all: their taste for and attraction to violence, which was something I couldn't comprehend at all.

A big help in getting to know groups of teenage lads and their girlfriends was plainly the fact that I was working for Granada TV in Manchester at the time. The lads got some kind of buzz, I suppose, from going to the pub with a bloke they'd seen on television presenting a weekly arts and entertainments programme called *What's On*.

From the start I was completely open and honest with them: I told them I was gathering material for a book, a work of fiction. Anything they revealed to me was in strict confidence. None of

them would be identified, either by name or description. They did-
n't object, in fact quite the reverse. I think they felt flattered that
someone was prepared to take an interest, to ask their opinions and
listen to their views on the world. I made one early mistake though.
I took along a pocket tape-recorder to the pub, and we all know
what happens to even garrulous people when they see they're being
recorded: they either clam up or they become wooden and self-con-
scious. From then on I left the tape-recorder behind, which meant
I had to wait several hours until I got home — often after midnight,
with three or four pints of John Willie Lees sloshing inside me —
to scribble down everything I could remember of the evening's conversation. I did this with different groups over a period of months,
drinking in pubs and clubs. From this material I started making
notes, trying to work out a structure or a shape for the book. I had
a bunch of characters in mind but only a vague notion of what
might happen to them, or even to the leading character, Kenny
Seddon. This was intentional. The kind of novel I had in mind
wouldn't work if it was too tightly structured, following too rigid a
plot-line. It needed room to breathe: a freedom and a flexibility to
go wherever the people in the story seemed to be heading, rather
than making them jump through so many dramatic hoops. (In
present-day publishing editor's jargon, 'character-led' rather than
'plot-driven'.)

From the moment I sat down to write it, I felt I'd caught the
right tone for the book. This is very much a hit-or-miss matter; you
need good luck as much as good judgement. I believe a writer
should trust his gut instinct and not get too intellectually hung up
about the process of creation — in my case for fear that it will place
the dead hand of some kind of orthodox or politically correct view-
point over the whole enterprise. (Of course the term 'politically correct' was unknown in 1975, but even then there were 'acceptable'
and 'correct' moral attitudes, particularly as regards young people,

it was worth ignoring and defying for the hell of it.) Also, I must have sensed that with subject matter this controversial and inflammatory — the cult of the skinhead, football hooliganism, racism, mindless *Clockwork Orange*-style violence, working-class life at the bottom of the barrel, the crude language of the streets — that to offset and downplay all of this, the writing had to be restrained, the style calm and matter-of-fact, almost documentary in approach.

Some time later I came across a remark of Evelyn Waugh's (a writer I very much admire), who in discussing fiction technique said something along the lines of: 'The hotter the emotion, the cooler the prose,' which summed up perfectly what I had been aiming for in this novel.

. . . .

When the book came out, Ed Teague, a friend of mine, held a small launch party at his bookshop on Yorkshire Street in Rochdale. Because of the book's subject matter, and the fact that Kenny Seddon ends up in Buckley Hall, the local youth detention centre (now a women's prison), Ed invited along members of the probation service. During the course of the evening, as we sipped wine and nibbled cheese, two, or it might have been three, probation officers sidled up and murmured in my ear that they could identify, without a shadow of doubt, the actual person that Kenny was based on. Each gave me the lad's name they were confident was the real Kenny — and each one was different. This demonstrated, I like to think, that the fictional character had sufficient depth and authenticity to convince them that they had encountered and had to deal with Kenny's real-life counterpart. They couldn't have done anyway. Kenny Seddon wasn't any particular person, he was a pick 'n' mix of several individuals. And the final character on the page was as much a product of the imagination as a portrait of anyone I met during my nights in the pub. I was a writer, not a journalist, and that's what writers are supposed to do.

The Ashfield Valley estate, a very unlovely group of buildings as you'll have gathered, was flattened in the late Eighties, though it wouldn't surprise me to learn that the council is still paying back the loan that built the 'San Quentin of the North', plus whacking great interest charges to boot. Even when relatively new, at the time Kenny Seddon's family lived there, they struck a chill to the heart. The piece of graffito I opened the book with — 'If you get caught in here God help you lousy scum' — wasn't my invention, it was scrawled on a wall at the bottom of a concrete stairwell.

A year or so after the book came out there was interest from a television company in making a film of it. I remember taking the producer and director on a tour of the actual locations: Ashfield Valley, town-centre pubs, Tweedale Street (where the mugging of the Pakistani happens in the book). They seemed genuinely enthusiastic, and for a few months it looked as if we were going ahead, but as is the way with the majority of such projects, talk is cheap and in the end nothing came of it. I'm pleased that the book is being reissued after this length of time — it's one I'm still rather proud of — to what is literally a new generation of readers. Strange to consider that Kenny and his mates will be in their mid-forties now, with teenage kids of their own ...

For those too young to remember, in the Seventies you'd see slogans sprayed all over the place with the word 'Rule' in them, as in 'Ashfield Skins Rule OK'. Hence the title, which I think fits the book well.

As for Buckley Hall, which I was given a tour of (courtesy of the Home Office), I was told years later by somebody who'd taught there that they had half-a-dozen copies of *Rule of Night* in the library. The book was a big favourite, apparently, much in demand by the teenage inmates, most of whom never read anything except

The Sun and maybe the racing results; very popular until all the copies got nicked. What I like to think of as literary criticism in action, and possibly the most flattering response I've had yet to any of my books.

Trevor Hoyle
Spring, 2003

POMONA BOOKS

POMONA'S AIM IS TO PRODUCE A CLASSIC BRANDING OF TITLES, each of them beautifully presented and immediately identifiable to readers. We will publish the work of stimulating and talented authors. Collect 'em all; feed your head.

Also available:

FOOTNOTE*
by Boff Whalley

ISBN 1-904590-00-4

FOOTNOTE IS CLEVER, FUNNY AND IRREVERENT — A STORY ABOUT A boy from the redbrick clichés of smalltown England reconciling Mormonism and punk rock, industrial courtesy and political insurrection.

He finds a guitar, anarchism and art terrorism and, after years (and years and years) of earnest, determined, honest-to-goodness slogging, his pop group† makes it big; that's BIG with a megaphone actually. They write a song that has the whole world singing and, funnily enough, it's an admirable summary of a life well lived — about getting knocked down and getting back up again.

Meanwhile, there's a whole world still happening: authentic lives carefully drawn, emotional but not sentimental and always with a writer's eye for detail. *Footnote* is not another plodding rock memoir but a compassionate, critical and sometimes cynical account of a life steeped in pop culture, lower division football and putting the world to rights.

---

* See page 293 of Boff Whalley's book.

† Boff Whalley is a member of Chumbawamba.

POMONA SOUNDS

SUCH IS OUR COMMITTMENT TO HARD WORK, IDEALISM AND the delivery of admirable products, Pomona Sounds is our affiliated record label.

The following CD albums will enhance your life:

PS-001	The Rosenbergs *Ameripop*
PS-002	Black September *Black September*
PS-003	Mudskipper *Eggshells*
PS-004	The Monkey Run *Escape From The Rake*
PS-005	Crass *You'll Ruin It For Everyone*
PS-006	Killing Stars *When The Light First Fell*
PS-007	Black September *You Can Do Anything If You Set Your Mind To It*

These albums should be available through your friendly local record store. If yours isn't so friendly, check out our website for more details: www.pomonasounds.co.uk.